"I'm not his be

"Sir, I cannot allow you to accost the lady in such a manner, betrothed or no. She denies your claim, so again, I must insist you release her." The lieutenant's hand moved to his sword, and I watched the margrave follow his movement as well. Most of the men at the party wore ordinary jackets, vests, pants, and high boots, but Culver was in uniform, complete with weaponry.

"Lady Prudence, we *will* continue this discussion at a later time when you have calmed down." He finally released my wrist, and I clutched it to myself, rubbing feeling back into my hand. "I suggest you make arrangements to accompany me in a few weeks when we head back to the continent." He took the path that returned to the house, and after retrieving her fork, Bobbie quietly followed him, giving me a cheesy thumbs-up and a wink. Strangely, while the margrave barely registered her presence, Culver gave her an odd look and watched while she departed.

"Lady Prudence, are you unharmed?" he asked me once Bobbie had disappeared.

"Yes, I'm all right. Thank you for coming to my rescue." It chafed a little to play the damsel in distress. Having not actually read this part, I was unsure of what to say next. Luckily, it looked like it was his line anyway.

"It is a great pleasure to see you again, though the circumstance were once again unpleasant. Do you often find yourself in peril?" He handed me the slipper I'd lost on the path.

"Not until very recently," I mumbled.

Penny Gothic: a romance of fictitious proportions

by

Shelley White

In for a Penny, Book 1

Penny Gothic: a romance of fictitious proportions

Cover Art by *Debbie Taylor*

The Wild Rose Press, Inc.
PO Box 708
Adams Basin, NY 14410-0708
Visit us at www.thewildrosepress.com

Publishing History
First Edition, 2021
Trade Paperback ISBN 978-1-5092-3789-0
Digital ISBN 978-1-5092-3790-6

Published in the United States of America

Dedication

To John, my personal romantic hero.
To my critique group: Richard, Susan,
Nelda, & Christina.
To Angela, beta reader extraordinaire.

Chapter 1

In Which I Inherit a Shabby Bookstore

"It's so cute!" Bobbie squealed as I closed the door behind me. We were standing in the foyer of my brand new (to me) used bookstore I had recently inherited from my gram. Disturbed dust motes swirled through the air, making themselves visible in the sun's scant rays, before settling back down on the dusty stacks of books covering every surface.

"Cute? Is that the best you can come up with for a description? I'm disappointed," I said as I wandered through the shop, turning on the various lamps my grandmother had used for ambiance.

"Cute, adorable, quaint, charming, delightful, winsome," Bobbie listed, gazing around the space. "Is that descriptive enough for you, Miss Penny Pincher?"

I cringed at the moniker. Yes, we were standing in Penny Pincher Used Books, and yes, my name was Penny (Penelope, actually), and yes, my grandmother, to my horror, named her late-in-life acquisition after her only granddaughter.

"That's Miss Darling to you if you plan to be my employee," I shot back. I used the term employee pretty loosely. At this point, I had no idea if the shop was even capable of turning a profit, let alone paying an employee. I'd promised Gram I'd keep it open for a year after her death and give it an honest effort. She'd been gone almost a month, and this was the first time I'd worked up the courage to visit her beloved bookstore.

Enter loyal friend, Bobbie Benton, who finally made me drag her down to see my inheritance; she's a bit of a bibliophile and is the smartest person I know. Bobbie volunteered to help me run the dusty shop in her spare time and volun-told her boyfriend Peter to pitch in as well in exchange for free books (for her) and coffee (for both).

My gram, Mabel Baker, passed away after a blessedly short battle with cancer. My grandpop died twelve years ago. My memories of him include walks in the woods, fishing, and pistachio ice cream. After he passed, Gram sold their house and bought this dinky little shop near the center of town.

It used to be an antique shop, and she bought the place lock, stock, and barrel. She opened it back up immediately and started selling off the antiques and filling shelves with used books. The random lamps, and few other un-sellably unique items, were all that remained of the antiques.

I used to spend afternoons here with Gram, helping out. She'd let me dust and sometimes ring up sales. We'd take English high tea with Mr. McKay from the shop next door if business was slow. I can't believe how many years I'd let slip by without a visit. Gram closed the shop when she first got sick six months ago, and there was never a reason for me to come by. An embarrassing layer of neglect covered everything.

"Well, that's awkwardly phrased," Bobbie announced. I turned to see Bobbie, hands on petite hips, glaring at the cornice above the check-out counter. Artfully written there in big, loopy font was "Discover your love in books."

"What's wrong with it? It's been there forever."

"Shouldn't it say, 'Discover a love of books' or 'Discover a love of reading' or something like that? It bothers my delicate sensibilities." She put her hand to her forehead in mock distress. "Even the overused 'Fall in love with a good book' would be better than that."

Bobbie reads *everything*. I'm not even kidding; everything from raunchy romances to eighteenth century political commentaries. The only place she draws the line is at bad writing. "I don't have time to waste on poor plot structure," she always says.

"It's not even catchy," she continued. "It doesn't really even work as a clever metaphor."

"Well, look at it this way." I stepped behind the counter. "You can't see it from back here where you'll be working." I winked at her, and she made a scrunchy face at me.

The jangle of the doorbell interrupted what was probably going to be a debate over fake quote wall decor.

"Knock, knock," Peter called. "Hey, this place is cool."

"Hey, babe," Bobbie said, moving in for a smooch and a squeeze, "how was practice?"

Peter scooped Bobbie up into a bear hug and gave her a wet peck on the cheek (gag!). They were about as mismatched as a couple could be. Where Bobbie was tiny, bookish, and well put-together, Peter was at least six-five, athletic, and tended to be sloppy. Their common ground was their utter devotion to each other.

Bobbie was studying for her master's degree in English literature at NCU, and Peter graduated last year with a degree in physical education and a minor in history. They've been dating since high school, and even though I knew Peter a little through our grandmothers, I didn't become friends with them both until our freshman year at NCU.

I, too, graduated last year with a bachelor's in business administration that I didn't think I'd ever use. It was something to appease my parents while I figured out what I really wanted to do. It looked like the joke was on me and I'd make use of the most boring degree in the world after all.

Though I liked to think of myself as "successfully single," the couple's frequent, cutesy PDAs made me want to throw up a little, but also made me uncomfortably jealous. Not that I had any designs on Peter, yuck, but I couldn't help but envy their relationship a little.

"Practice was fine. Coach is getting ready to make cuts; it's going to be brutal." Peter was lucky to get a job last fall as a special ed teacher's assistant at the local high school and also assistant basketball coach. He's hoping to be first in line if any openings become available in PE or history. He finally set Bobbie back on her feet with a playful tug on her perfect braid.

"That will make practices easier though," Bobbie said. "I don't know how you even get anything accomplished with fifty-four boys."

"True that," Peter agreed. "So show me around your little shop of horrors."

Bobbie grabbed his hand to do the honors and dragged him through the aisles. I turned to the antique

4

cash register and began taking inventory of what I had to work with.

****

My alarm clock screamed. I reluctantly pulled myself out of a most delightful dream. Gram and I were sitting on a bench in the park. A breeze was blowing my auburn curls lightly across my face. Gram was wearing her blue head scarf with the ladybugs. We were eating pistachio ice cream cones.

"You'll find him, of course. Just like I did."

"Of course!" I agreed enthusiastically. My waking self had no idea what I had agreed to, but dream-me seemed good to go.

"Just be careful. And read my letters," Gram said as a giant vulture pigeon swooped out of the sky and grabbed my ice cream. Okay, so maybe the whole dream wasn't delightful. But it was nice to see Gram looking so healthy, even if it was only in my sleep. It, at least, put me in the right mood to go back to the bookstore today.

Bobbie and I had spent all Saturday dusting bookshelves and lamps (there were fifteen!). Today, after church, we were planning to tackle the back room. I would have to pray for fortitude.

The back room was stuffed from wall to wall and almost floor to ceiling with estate sale fodder and well-meaning donations, all covered in dust. The whole place was due for a good weeding, but I didn't dare get rid of anything till I knew what Gram's clientele preferred.

In Gram's paperwork I found enough information to reassure me that the shop almost always broke even, and some months actually made a profit. But I didn't find any type of sales record or inventory list to know what had been sold. There was a customer list, at least, that I intended to utilize to announce my grand re-opening, but other than that, nada.

I had decided to take over Gram's old apartment upstairs to save on expenses in case the shop was a money pit. I'd left my job in Atlanta and found someone to take over my lease. I intended to really give this some effort.

My parents lived in Atlanta, too. My mom stuck around for a couple weeks after the funeral to help me move in upstairs. She's an interior designer with high-end clientele, so my grandmother knew she'd never want to be saddled with a decrepit little book shop. Mom and Dad were very supportive of my inheriting the old place. So supportive, they could hardly contain the looks of relief on their faces when they heard. Dad is a copy editor and needed to be in the city for work as well.

The apartment had a separate entrance in the back alley and an inconspicuous stairway behind a locked door in the shop, handy if I needed to run downstairs to say, grab my forgotten e-reader.

Oh, the irony. I haven't cracked open a real book since graduation last May, preferring to download books from the library or online. Now I find myself the proud owner of an eclectic mix of moldering, silverfish-infested hardback treasures.

Also, my preferred genre is contemporary fantasy fiction. I don't know anything about most (probably all) of my inventory. Hopefully the customers are used to helping themselves.

I crawled out of bed, leaving behind the little

Gram-shaped hollow I'd been snuggled in. I'd inherited all of Gram's personal belongings as well: the bedding that smelled like her linen closet, her apple dishes, and enough polyester to clothe the entire homeless population of Upper Orrington. The former was packed up in the six boxes stacked by the door waiting for someday when I finally remember to donate them to Mary & Martha House thrift store.

I staggered to the bathroom, gripped the sink, and faced myself in the mirror. The gentle breeze from my dream looked to have been a hurricane in actuality. There was no saving my hair this morning without a shower.

After a lukewarm shower and cold rinse, I found my least-wrinkled shirt and favorite jeans, tackled my hair into submission, slipped on my short boots, and headed out the door. Usually, I could count on Bobbie to supply Sunday morning caffeine, and today was no exception.

I was looking forward to worship. Hopefully, it would inspire me today and put me in the mood to clean out the cobwebs this afternoon.

****

"More encyclopedias." I sat down on a box with a huff. We'd been working for three hours, assessing and recording the contents of a million dusty boxes.

"Maybe we could donate them to the high school," Bobbie suggested.

"I think these are *from* the high school, actually," I replied, looking at the stickers on the side of the box.

"That brings us up to four sets so far. There's some good stuff here too, though. Quite a few cookbooks— they're timeless, Christian romance, and a collection of local yearbooks dating from 1950-1965," Bobbie listed.

"I'm not sure how much of that qualifies as 'good stuff,' but I think the 'bad stuff' outweighs it. *'DOS for Dummies'* anyone? How about some 1970s *National Geographic*?" I countered. "At least we've made a path to the back shelves."

"Do you think the really good stuff is back there?"

I laughed. "No, it just seemed important to set a goal for today."

A metallic knock and a muffled, "Are you guys back there?" sounded from the storeroom delivery door.

"That's Peter," said Bobbie, brightening, she attempted to brush the dust out of her chocolate brown hair. I weaved my way back through the labyrinth of boxes to unlock the back door for Peter and, to my amusement, his grandmother, Biddy.

Her name is actually Estelle. I'm not sure where the name Biddy came from, other than the woman looks way more like a "Biddy" than an "Estelle." Everyone not related to her calls her Aunt Biddy.

"Hey guys," said Peter. He led Biddy in through the service door. "After dinner Biddy wanted to come see the shop. I didn't think you'd mind, Pen."

Peter took his grandma to dinner every Sunday. Since she's in her late seventies, they usually manage to hit senior rush hour at most restaurants around four p.m. It's very sweet, and I keep telling Bobbie that grandma-care is an excellent quality to look for in a potential spouse. Not that she needs me to point out Peter's finer qualities, but I like to tease.

"Not at all," I replied. "Just mind the dust. It's a mess, but we're slowly working through it."

"Oh, I don't mind a bit of dust, sweetie. Mabel and

I spent many an afternoon back here sorting books. I do miss her," she said sadly.

"I do, too," I agreed, putting my arm around her narrow shoulders. She patted me on the back and gave me a mischievous grin.

"So, have you read any of them yet?" she asked with a weird, penetrating gleam in her eye.

"Oh, no," I answered. "None of these are really my style; I don't know that there's anything in this entire shop I'd be interested in. As long as the customers like it..."

"What a shame," Biddy mused, scanning the piles of books we had been inventorying, "You should really give some of these a try. You might be surprised." There was that gleam in her eye again.

Biddy really did remind me a lot of Gram. They had been friends since high school and told me some pretty wild stories from their youth. Of course, 1950s-wild was pretty tame by today's standards, but I always managed to look appropriately shocked when Gram started reminiscing.

"I suppose I will at some point," I conceded, following her gaze. "I'll have to familiarize myself with my inventory if I want to be an effective salesperson."

Biddy gave me an assessing look that lasted about two beats, gave a sharp nod, as if to say, "you'll do," and headed back toward the door.

"Let me know if you need any help," she called over her shoulder. "I used to help Mabel a bit now and then." She turned to Peter. "I'm ready to go home. Petey, my show's coming on soon."

"Yes, ma'am," he said, then turned to Bobbie and me. "I'll be back in twenty minutes to move this stuff wherever you need."

"Nah, don't worry about it. We won't get any more done tonight anyway. Besides, I'm ready to crash. Why don't you take Bobbie out? She's been a trooper."

"Come with us," Bobbie pleaded. "You've been working just as hard."

"No thanks," I begged off. "I've already got plans with a hot shower and Chinese takeout. Can you come by after classes tomorrow? I should have it somewhat organized by then, and you can help me with decision-making. Peter, I will probably be able to use the muscle you offered on Thursday to haul off the stuff we decide not to keep. I really want to be open by Saturday."

"Okay, I'll be back in a bit to get you, Bobbie." He gave her filthy clothes a once-over. "We'll go someplace casual," he told her with a wink.

"Goodnight, girls. Be sure to call me if you have any questions, Penelope," Biddy reminded me.

"Goodnight, Aunt Biddy," Bobbie and I chimed. "Thanks for coming by. It's always good to see you," I added.

She waved us off, and Peter followed her, shutting the door behind them.

I turned back to Bobbie, who was uselessly trying to brush the dust from her pants.

"So now that we made it this far, *are* there any treasures on that shelf?" I wondered aloud, meeting her at the end of the path. "I promise we won't inventory. I just want to peek in those boxes before you have to leave. Maybe there will be some reward for our efforts today," I added hopefully.

The boxes on the shelf did not look at all like the newer acquisitions. They were much dustier and a couple, I noticed, were addressed to the old antique shop. They might not even contain books, just old leftovers.

Bobbie squeezed into the space to look over my shoulder. "These are *really* dusty." She sniffed and blew her nose on a tissue from her pocket. "Well, open it up; if it's super old, maybe it will have some value and we can sell it on eBay and retire in Cancun."

I pulled one of the boxes toward me and carefully unfolded the lid, trying not to disturb the thick dust.

"It's another lamp! Good grief, what was wrong with this one that it didn't rate the front of the shop? Looks equally ugly to the others to me." I refolded the box and shoved it aside. I reached farther back and pulled another box forward. It was heavier, thus more promising. I unfolded this one a little less gently, sending dust everywhere and causing Bobbie to step back.

Inside this box were three stacks of really old looking, thin, paperback-type books. "Now these might be something." I lifted one from the top of a stack. "They look old enough to be worth something, and they're in pretty good shape, too, other than some major yellowing."

"Oooh! Do you know what those are?" she asked excitedly. "They're penny-bloods."

I gave her a blank look, so she continued.

"Penny dreadfuls? Penny goths?" She gave a huff and a sigh. "How do you not know this? They are Victorian-era fiction that sold in installments for a penny each, hence the nickname."

"What about the blood and dreadful parts?" I asked, studying the book in my hand more closely.

"They weren't necessarily quality literature. They started out as 'true crime' stories based on local crimes and murders. Eventually, they took on a life of their own and publishers began printing original, fictional publications. They were gothic horrors or romances, the bloodier, the better. Remember that play we saw, *Sweeny Todd*?"

"The one based on the much better Johnny Depp movie?" I recalled.

Bobbie gave me a disappointed look. "Yes, that story was an original penny publication."

"Ah, I see. That story was warped. I hope it was fiction and not true crime." I shuddered.

"They weren't all like that. The scandalous romances were pretty popular too. They also turned American Wild West stories into penny pubs. Think of them like Victorian-era dime novels." Bobbie was warming up to her subject now. "They would probably be worth more in England than here. Maybe you could try eBay. I know there's got to be collectors out there that would love to find so many in such great condition."

I read the cover of the book in my hand, "*The Murderous Margrave*, ooh, sounds titillating." I opened it somewhere in the middle.

"Be careful! They weren't well-made to begin with. You don't want to damage the merchandise."

"I'll be gentle. What's a 'margrave' anyway? Sounds regal."

"A margrave was originally the medieval title for a military commander for the Holy Roman Empire, the area that is now Germany and Austria. The job and title passed down from father to son, but they stopped using it around 1800."

"Well, maybe this is…" I scanned the cover for the author's name. "P.L. Delphine's attempt at historical fiction. How do you even know all that anyway? You sound like an encyclopedia."

Bobbie shrugged. "You know, I just remember things. I think it was from helping Peter study for a Euro history test a couple years ago."

I skimmed a few lines, taking a moment to adjust to the antique print and writing style. "Oh, my. Listen to this, it sounds like a really bad Harlequin."

Chapter 2

In Which I Have a Nightmare While Totally Awake

The Murderous Margrave

When the ball came to a close, Lady Prudence and Lady Seraphina waited in the parlor for their wraps to be retrieved, then descended the marble stairs to their awaiting coach. Lady Prudence was quite overcome from the stimulation and near-ruinous events that had taken place. She was only too grateful that no persons had been in the vicinity to witness her untimely encounter.

She craved nothing more than to settle into the plush seats of their conveyance and rest her weary eyelids until they arrived back at Bellweather Manor. Lady Seraphina, unattuned to Lady Prudence's distress, had no such desideratum.

"Lady Prudence, was that not a most pleasurably diverting evening? I was taken 'round by no fewer than twenty different escorts, though barely three held the pedigree my father requires in a suitor. What of the margrave? Did I not observe you in conversation with him on several occasions? I would not be surprised if an offer was not forthcoming. Certainly, your stepfather would be most pleased with such a match."

Lady Prudence did wish that Lady Seraphina

would cease nattering on, but as hostess, felt compelled to forego her rest and participate in the speculation her friend so obviously had planned.

"Lady Seraphina, please know that I would never seek out such a match nor attempt to encourage the margrave's attentions. He is naught but a scoundrel and a blackguard and pursues me despite my disdain for him. He lives nearby the town which my stepfather is from and is known to my family. Though he has a reputation of a rogue and a villain, my stepfather continues to promote a match due to the boon such a relationship would bring him.

"It is my good fortune that my father left me such a sizable inheritance when he died that I have the luxury to choose a husband for myself."

The coach had started on its way after sitting in the queue behind several ahead of it. Lady Seraphina leaned forward in order to be heard over the noise of the wheels while still maintaining a polite level of speech.

"Indeed, I have not heard of any black marks on the margrave's reputation in this part of the country. Surely a gentleman such as himself is merely looking for an opportunity to settle down with a lady such as yourself who would not only bring refinement to his home but also prosperity through your stepfather's connections. Surely, much can be overlooked when there is a title to be gained," Lady Seraphina wheedled, always a practical thinker.

"That may be true," Lady Prudence replied, "but after this evening I am even more unwavering in my commitment to spurn the margrave's suit. He dogged my heels all evening and did his utmost to dissuade any other gentleman who dared approach me.

"I will tell you this in the strictest confidence because it has me unduly distressed and quite vexed. At one point in the evening, I was feeling so overcome by the heat created by all the bodies enjoying the festivities, I stepped out on the veranda for some respite. I was quite alone and thankful that I was not required to make polite conversation with other guests who might have been in the proximity.

"As I was about to re-enter the hall the curtain parted, and the margrave joined me on the veranda. He did not even pretend he was unaware of my presence, a subterfuge that would not have worked in any event. He stepped very close to my person, close enough that if we had been discovered I would have been ruined. He stated that my stepfather had already agreed to a marriage between us and that I should consider us betrothed. I said that I would consider no such thing and asked that he step aside so that I may return to the ball.

"He then attempted to force his attentions on me and would have if not for my quick thinking and my fan. I stepped around him and made my way to the door. He said, 'Do not think that you can deny me what has been promised. One way or another, you will become my wife. Willing or unwilling, it matters little to me.' Then he smiled at me in the most evil manner. I did not wait for him to say more but hastened to find you so that we could make a swift departure."

"Oh, Lady Prudence! How dreadful to have been exposed to such base behavior. That man is no gentleman, despite his lofty title. Please accept my deepest apologies for encouraging a match between you. Whatever do you plan to do if he continues his pursuit? What will your stepfather say when he learns of your denial?"

"I am not over-worried about my stepfather, Sir Reginald. Even if he chose to disown me, there are plenty of people who remember my father and would offer me aid. Father was of much higher rank in society. I do understand my mother's loneliness after my father's death, but she should not have lowered herself so in her remarriage."

"Let us not think about it anymore. It will be another month before we are required to return to London for the pre-season assemblies. It was most fortuitous that you were included in Lady Winchell's house party guest list. Why, with all of the entertainments and offerings provided here, we shan't even miss the city, and you will not have to face Sir Reginald for weeks."

"I just hope the margrave will not be a continued presence at any more outings," Lady Prudence said darkly.

Suddenly, the carriage lurched, causing both passengers to clutch the plush arm holds. It then proceeded to pick up speed.

Lady Prudence gasped, wondering at the sudden increase in momentum. Lady Seraphina's elegantly coiffed twist had somehow come undone and was now hanging in an unfathomable braid over her shoulder, and she was wearing spectacles!

Lady Prudence was most confused. The tumultuous ride was making it impossible for her to think clearly. Her own unruly auburn locks were bouncing about her face, adding to her disorientation as she did not, to her knowledge, possess auburn curls.

Lady Seraphina exclaimed, "What the heck is going on?" in a most undignified, peasant-like manner, causing Lady Prudence to question the wisdom of inviting her slightly lower-in-station friend to such an esteemed invitation-only house party.

Lady Penelope was only distracted by Lady Bobbie's unbecoming outburst for a moment before realizing she was no longer covered in dust and her face was caked with an inordinate amount of makeup. Her stays were digging into her back most uncomfortably and the bodice of her dress was beginning to itch. Lady Penelope found she had no recollection of donning the irritating, yet fine garment when she readied herself for church that morning. "What perplexing circumstances," she thought to herself.

"Pen, snap out of it! I really need you with me!" Lady Bobbie's demanding tone finally broke through the fog Lady Penelope found herself...myself in...

"Pen, Penelope! Are you with me? Cause I really need you to tell me I'm not in the middle of this nightmare alone."

Bobbie. It was Bobbie across from me, not Lady Bobbie, or Lady Sara-whats-it, I was Penny, not Lady Prudence. Yet somehow, I still was, because, Toto, we weren't in Kansas anymore.

Chapter 3

In Which I Assess the Situation

Time to assess the situation, real quick-like. Bobbie
and I were possibly having the same nightmare. We
were bouncing around in what felt like a runaway
stagecoach instead of the dusty storage room. We were
wearing hideously heavy ball gowns and, I wiggled in
my seat, no panties!

"I'm here, I'm with you. What's going on?" I
asked as we continued to be tossed around. Bobbie gave
me an exasperated look.

"Don't ask me, I think it's your nightmare, not
mine. Do something, be in charge, I don't know,
change something!"

"Um, stagecoach, stop!" I shouted at the ceiling.
Nothing. "Please, stop?" I said more politely.

"Maybe you're not calling it the right thing. Based
on our clothes and this fancy interior, I don't think this
is a wild West stagecoach. Try calling it a carriage."

"Let's try it together, just in case this is your
dream, since you seem to know so much about it."

"Fine."

"Carriage, please stop," we shouted together, to no
avail.

"Let's open the slidey window thing," I suggested.
"I can't even tell what time of day it is."

Bobbie opened the window on the door. "Definitely nighttime. Looks like we're in the woods."

I opened the window behind me. "Yep, nighttime, woods, and a guy on a big black horse chasing us."

Bobbie crossed to sit next to me and peer out the window.

"Is he rescuing or chasing?" she asked.

"I came in at the same time you did. I have no idea, but I'm voting for rescue." I lifted my acreage of skirts so I could climb up on my knees and stuck my arm out the window. "Hey! You there on the horse, help us," I yelled as I waved my arm.

"Mi'lady, I must insist you secure your arm inside the carriage. Tis not safe!"

"Peter?!" Bobbie said incredulously to the face that had just appeared outside our window.

"Bobbie?" Peter blinked in confusion. "What am I doing?"

"You appear to be our footman. Just hang on, okay. We don't know what's going on, we might be dreaming, but right now we're just trying to stop this runaway coach."

"Carriage," I corrected, helpfully. I was thankful and impressed with Peter's athleticism. Bobbie and I could hardly keep our seats, it had to be rougher on the outside.

"Um," Peter said. "I don't think you want to stop."

"Of course, we want to stop. I was trying to get that rider's attention so he could help us."

Peter squinted and peered through the fog that had slowly crept in around them. "Penny, that dude is wearing a mask and sporting a rifle. I don't think his plan is to help you."

"Crap!" I sat back on my haunches.

"Woohoo! I haven't had this much fun in years!"

Bobbie and I spun around as fast as our dresses would allow, Bobbie nearly toppling in the process.

"Biddy?" Peter exclaimed through the open window. His grandmother was ensconced in the seat Bobbie had recently vacated.

"None other, Sweetie. Girls, just settle down and enjoy the ride. I'm sure he'll be along in a moment. Petey, do hang on, will you? I don't think you can die, but a fall will certainly cause you to wake up sore."

We all just stared at her, dumbfounded. She apparently found the perfect center of the carriage because she wasn't bouncing near as much as we were. She, too, was turned out in an extravagantly ugly ball gown. Poor Peter. It had a scandalous neckline that nobody should have to witness on his Granny.

"Aunt Biddy, do you know what's going on?" I asked.

"Of course, Penelope. It's your legacy, you lucky girl!" She smiled, as if I should be excited about any of this.

"See, I knew this wasn't my fault," Bobbie said with the confidence of someone who is often right.

"Ladies, we have another rider on our tail," Peter said from the window.

"Yes, that'll be him," Aunt Biddy said serenely.

"Who?" I asked. Bobbie and I returned to our knees to observe this new development.

"You'll see," she replied mysteriously.

Outside, we watched as a second horse and rider emerged from the mist and galloped up beside the first. This horse was pearl gray in the moonlight and a taller, leaner breed than the first. The rider wasn't masked. I couldn't see his face well, but his hair was light, and his clothes appeared to be a uniform of sorts, red coat, buff pants, and tall black boots.

When the dark rider noticed him, he spurred his own mount forward trying to gain us before having to encounter the newcomer. But he was clearly outmatched. As the new rider quickly closed the distance, the masked rider decided to cut his losses. He peeled-off into the woods and was absorbed into the darkness.

Peter reached around and pounded on the hard side of the carriage wall. "Hey! Driver! Slow up!"

Finally, we slowed. Our rescuer caught up to us and rode at our flank until we came to a complete stop. Peter hopped down and came around to our door, opened it, and helped us down the narrow step, assisting Biddy first.

"Man, thanks for the help, I didn't have a clue how we were going to get out of that." Peter offered a handshake.

The man, who I could now see had wavy blond hair, sun-bronzed skin, and piercing eyes that were so dark blue, they were almost black, looked at Peter in confusion.

Biddy rapped Peter on the wrist with her folded fan (did she even have a fan a few minutes ago?)

"Shush, Petey. The help doesn't speak, besides you're not a main character."

Peter stepped back, and the man turned to address me. "Milady, I trust you are unscathed."

Biddy's elbow jabbed into my waist.

"Uh, yes, we're fine," I stammered. He grasped my

hand, brought it to his lips and bowed slightly as he barely kissed the back of my gloved hand.

"It would be my privilege to escort you to your destination."

"Um, I'm not even sure where we are, let alone where we're going," I managed to say.

"This is Yorkshire, my home. I've just returned this evening from serving with my unit on the continent. First Lieutenant Culver Eberhart, at your service." He actually clicked his heels together when he released my hand. He smiled at me then, and it almost took my breath away. His lips curved and a single dimple appeared on his right cheek. His teeth were nearly as perfect as the rest of him, but for an upper canine, slightly askew.

His straight nose and strong jawline, added to the rest, made the lieutenant exactly the man of my dreams, literately and figuratively, apparently. All I could do was stare at him, speechless again.

His horse nickered and drew my attention. Being a reformed horse-crazy tween, I recognized his gorgeous dappled gray mare was a Lipizzaner. Man and horse together were impressive, I'd even go so far to say, swoon-worthy.

"Thank you, Lieutenant," Biddy said, stepping in when words failed me. "Of course, she knows where she's going, she's simply overwrought. The driver has our direction. We don't want to keep you from your homecoming but are honored by your kind offer."

"Well then, allow me to help you get on your way."

He assisted Biddy into the coach, then Bobbie, while Peter looked on helplessly. Then he turned to assist me.

"This has already been a more pleasurable homecoming than I could have hoped for," he said, looking into my eyes, "Might you give me your name, that I may have something to call you when you haunt my dreams?"

I couldn't decide whether to swoon or laugh in his face. It was probably the worst pick-up line I'd ever heard, but somehow he made it work.

"I'm Penelope, Penny."

"Fair Lady Penelope." He kissed my hand again, this time closer to where my glove met the edge of my sleeve. A shiver raced up my arm. "Till we meet again." He delivered me up the steps (though I might have floated) and into the carriage, shutting the door firmly behind me.

Chapter 4

Where Everything Becomes Clear—But Not Really

"What just happened?!" I was stunned. We were suddenly back at the bookstore in our dusty clothes, the old book still in my hand, open.

"Achoo!" Bobbie sneezed, then sniffled. "Give me that!" She grabbed the book from my hand and started reading, "*Lady Prudence's heart was aflutter. She didn't know the blackguard who had pursued them, but she couldn't help but be exceedingly grateful to the ruthless cur. Without his pursuance, she would not have had the opportunity to meet the handsome lieutenant. It was truly lamentable that he was merely a lowly lieutenant. She would have to mention him to her hostess, Lady Bellweather, who was forever bewailing the lack of male partners at her dinners.*

"While he may not be suitable for marriage, no one would begrudge her a discreet flirtation." She pitched the book back in the box. "I knew you did that."

"What? I didn't do that. I don't even know what that was. Were we in the book?"

"Sure seemed like it to me!"

I'd never seen Bobbie so riled. We were interrupted by frantic pounding on the back door and a muffled, "Bobbie! Are you all right? Open up, let us in!" from Peter.

Bobbie shoved past me and hurried through the box maze to the door and yanked it open. Peter burst through and Bobbie launched herself into his arms. As he held her, Peter surveyed the area to make sure we were still in a bookshop in the twenty-first century. Biddy followed close behind.

"What a hoot!" she exclaimed, slapping her polyester-clad thigh, "I haven't had that much fun in years. Woo-whee!"

Biddy brought with her a welcome dose of reality, and it occurred to me that she was not nearly as shaken by the experience as a woman her age ought to be, or at all, really. And I bet she had some answers...

Bobbie seemed calmed by Peter's presence. Her well-ordered world had been seriously rocked.

"I don't suppose you can shed some light on the situation, Aunt Biddy?"

"Oh, girl! You have no idea, do you?" She gave me a pitying look. "Petey, go out front and put on some coffee—you kept Mabel's old machine, didn't you? It makes the best brew—we'll have us a sit down and a nice chat."

Biddy perched in the drab green wingback that dominated the reading nook. She looked like a queen presiding over the rest of us in our eclectic assortment of aesthetically challenged club chairs. Peter handed her a full mug, and she inhaled the aroma deeply.

"I'm missing my show for this, Petey. You'll have to find it for me later on the Hulu-tube thingy." She turned to me. "I can tell by the look on your face you haven't even read your gram's letters. Shame on you."

"What letters?" But her mention of them triggered something in the back of my memory. Last night's dream.

Biddy sighed, "Maybe she didn't have time to tell you about them. But I'm sure they are somewhere upstairs."

"I haven't had the time or the heart to go through everything yet, but Mom helped me pack up quite a bit of the upstairs before I moved in," I admitted.

Bobbie and Peter joined us with their coffees and handed me a mug that said BOOK-ISH.

"I can tell you the little bit I know, but your gram can explain it to you better—hence the letters." She settled in to begin her tale.

"I've known your gram since high school, you know that. Mabel and I were like sisters. I was almost as sad as she was when her grandmother passed away our senior year. She left Mabel a stack of letters, we poured through them together. The one on top was from her grandmother, Hazel, but each of the ones after that were from different women in her family, every other generation all the way back to 1783.

"So we started reading, and the story that unfolded was so unbelievable...but we were reading letters that were undeniably over one hundred years old. All personal versions of the same theme." We could all tell this was the climax of Biddy's story; she fanned her fingers in front of her and said, "Gypsy Magic," like she was stage magician.

"Penny's family is cursed by gypsies?" Bobbie asked skeptically. "That's not even a real thing."

"Babe, what happened this afternoon was totally real. I have a blister on my hand from hanging on so tight." Peter displayed his palm.

"Shush now, don't interrupt," Biddy admonished.

"It's not a curse."

"Could have fooled me," Bobbie huffed under her breath. Biddy ignored her and continued.

"Way back in the mid-seventeen hundreds, your ancestor, I don't remember her name, was unfortunate in love. I don't remember many details, or any, to be honest, other than she went to the gypsies and paid for a bit of magic. But before she could put the magic to use, she fell in love and married a man from the camp. The unused magic aged and warped a tiny bit and was somehow passed down to her own granddaughter. It's surfaced in every other generation since then."

"Warped how exactly?" I asked.

"Well, I can't say for sure, not knowing what the actual intent was, but it seems like your ancestress asked for a 'love like she read about in books.' And since then, every other generation has to find their own true love in a book. The end." Biddy sat back, satisfied with her story despite the numerous holes she left.

"That's crazy! There is no way in the world that can really happen to real people."

"Oh, you're probably right, but remember you've got that touch of gypsy in your blood. I'm sure it added a monkey wrench into how things were supposed to have played out. You'll have to allow for a little crazy."

"If this is her curse, how come we were all there?" Bobbie asked with a hint of resentment.

"How does it work, exactly?" I added.

"Well, I don't know how it works, of course. I'm no magic expert, but I can give you the gist of what happens. Your gram and I had such fun trying it out.

"Essentially, you read yourself into a book and everyone else in the vicinity goes along for the ride.

You meet your true love, get him to wake up and realize he's an actual person on the outside, then figure out how to connect in real life."

"You're saying that dishy lieutenant guy is my soul mate?" *So* not on my to-do list for today!

"Looks like! Lucky girl! It took Mabel and me several chapters to figure out who your grandpa was. But, then again, she started at the beginning and you jumped right to the middle, didn't you?" She wagged a "naughty girl" finger at me.

"What happens if she finishes the book before the guy has his self-realization?" Bobbie asked.

"Well, just start another book. He'll show up. It may take a couple, depending on how slowly he adjusts to the process."

"What happens out here while I'm gallivanting around in story land?"

"Nothing. No time passes at all, which is pretty lucky since your husband-to-be would have had a hard time explaining why he tended to check-out from time to time.

"Your grandfather said he never noticed it at first until he started to self-realize—to use your word, Bobbie, it's a good one—in the book. Then he said the episodes seemed like weird memories of dreams. In fact, he had himself convinced they were dreams until Mabel and I showed up where he worked one afternoon. I'll never forget the expression on David's face," she mused.

"After she met him, it stopped, right?"

"Oh no. The gift is yours until you die and pass it on to your granddaughter."

"If that's the case, how did anyone ever figure out

what caused it?" Bobbie asked, ever the practical one for details.

"Well, since the first gal wasn't using the magic, it passed immediately to her granddaughter on her fifteenth birthday. They were close, and between them and her husband's gypsy knowledge, they were able to piece together a theory. A theory that has proven pretty spot-on over the last century or so. That's why they all wrote the letters, to make it easier for the next girl."

"And my mom doesn't know any of this?"

"Your mom's a bit straitlaced. She would have a hard time believing something she didn't experience. Kind of like you." She peered at me over the top of her glasses. "Besides, there was no point, the legacy wasn't being passed to her anyway."

"Why didn't Gram just tell me?"

"Well, no one really expected the bit'o magic to last beyond the first granddaughter. Each generation kind of hopes to be the last. The letters have just been precautionary."

"Is there any way to control it, or am I just going to start jumping into every book I pick up?"

"Don't worry about that. There do seem to be a few loose rules. Once you start a book, you'll only be able to read yourself into that book until it's finished. Anything else you start after that time will be safe until you finish the first."

"Am I stuck jumping into books for the rest of my life?"

"As soon as you are wearing the first granddaughter's ring in marriage, you'll be able to stop. But only in marriage. It won't do anything for you now except look pretty."

"Why her ring and not the one who started the magic?"

"Because the first granddaughter found her true love. Her grandmother married the gypsy man. They loved each other well enough and had a reasonably happy life, but they weren't each other's true love."

"What about the guy who should have been my multiple great grandfather? Is he out there somewhere?"

"Well, I'm sure he's quite dead by now."

Bobbie threw her hands up in exasperated defeat.

"But there's a theory," Biddy continued, "no facts behind it whatsoever, mind you, but one of the past grandmothers suggested that when one of the granddaughters meets and marries one of the grandsons, the magic will be fulfilled."

"And the curse broken," I concluded.

Biddy scowled at me. "It's not a curse, girl."

"So if Penny's not ready to settle down and do the whole marriage thing, she just has to stop reading that book, right?" Bobbie asked. I could almost see her brain working on my behalf.

"She can try. Mabel got frustrated with the process a time or two and tried to quit. Even went out with a few beaus. But they never lasted long. None compared to David. A soul mate is a soul mate, after all."

I brought my now-cold coffee to my lips and frowned into my cup. "I guess I'd better find those letters and find a safe place for Gram's ring."

"She would have put them someplace where you would be sure to find them, and not your mother accidentally."

"Maybe in that box of bookstore paperwork we

haven't tackled yet," Bobbie suggested, heading to the check-out area to retrieve the box.

It had been dusted along with everything else but remained unopened. She dragged it out of the cabinet, then Peter carried it down and set it on the coffee table between us. My name was on top and it said "very important store papers" on the top. I stared at it in trepidation.

"Come on," Bobbie said, removing the lid. "Hopefully we'll find more answers."

Inside were stuffed manila file folders labeled with "taxes 2005-2010" and "Insurance." Bobbie lifted those out. Underneath was a gallon size Ziploc bag. "Penelope" was written on the outside in black marker. Beneath Gram's loopy cursive I could see the bag held a bundle of letters wrapped in a green ribbon and a bundle of photocopied pages clipped together. I lifted the bag out carefully.

"Some of the older letters were falling apart, so Mabel copied them for you," Biddy said from her chair.

These were from Gram; they felt personal. I suddenly felt very protective of them.

"I think I want to read these on my own. I'll share them with you tomorrow, I promise," I quickly added when a hurt look flashed across Bobbie's face. I'd inadvertently dragged her into this, so she deserved to see them, but I couldn't just yet.

"Bobbie, can you come over after your classes tomorrow? I just need to be alone with my gram tonight."

Bobbie nodded in understanding and gave me a tight hug. Peter was already rinsing out the mugs. They would exit the same way they came in so I wouldn't have to unlock the front door.

Biddy called over her shoulder as she disappeared out the back, "It will be easier to accept when you realize it's a gift and stop viewing it as a curse."

Bobbie finally released me from her hug and looked me in the eye. "You call me if you want me to come over. Any time of night, okay?"

"Absolutely," I reassured her.

Peter came over and collected Bobbie, patting me on the shoulder as he led her away. He'd been pretty quiet this afternoon, but that wasn't unusual for him. Besides, it was a lot for all of us to absorb.

Chapter 5

Ancestry Dot Me

I shut off the lamps and the light in the storeroom before heading upstairs. I had the bag of letters as well as three books that were at the bottom of the box, underneath the letters. They were old, and since Gram had included them, I figured they must be important. I was about halfway up the stairs to my apartment when I decided *The Murderous Margrave* now qualified as an "important book" in my new reality, so I rushed back down to retrieve it.

I showered, then decided I didn't want to see people, so opted to heat up a frozen pizza and forego the Chinese food.

While my pizza heated, I put on comfy clothes and lay everything out on my coffee table so I could contemplate it while I ate. I really wanted to start plowing through it, but I was also starved and wouldn't risk ruining anything with pizza grease.

The three books were *Breakfast at Tiffany's*, *Pride and Prejudice*, and, strangely enough, *The Holy Bible*. I placed them in a square with *The Murderous Margrave*.

Then I pulled out the photocopies and placed those next to the books. There appeared to be copies of every letter except Gram's, so I only pulled hers out of the beribboned bundle.

Should I read oldest to newest or start with Gram's and work backwards? I'd have to weigh the pros and cons of each method while I ate, I decided as the stove timer buzzed.

Hunger sated, I settled on Gram's letter since she was the only one who had written specifically to me. The envelope wasn't sealed, but my name was written on the front. It was almost like being able to talk to Gram again. Tears sprang to my eyes. She wasn't done giving me advice, and I sure wasn't done hearing it from her. I carefully unfolded three pages filled with her loopy scrawl.

June 2012

Penelope,

If you're reading this, I've finally received my great reward. I've so much to tell you that I wish I could have said in person, but I didn't want our time left together to be overwhelmed by the legacy. I wanted you to be my little Penny for a little while longer. Who knows, between now and my death I may change my mind, but since I have to write this letter for posterity anyway, here it is.

If I'm dead, you may already have discovered something odd happens when you read a book. If that's the case, I'm so sorry I didn't tell you sooner. In that event, don't panic. You are safe and no time actually passes while you are otherwise engaged.

If you are reading this before anything has happened, I'll try to prepare you...

I'm making a muddle of it. I'm so sorry. How about this, stop here and read Elizabeth's letter. It should be the top copy in the bundle.

****

Well, that was helpful, leave it to Gram to help me navigate through the order in which to read the letters. I unclipped the stack. The top four pages were gray, like when copies are made of pages that aren't white, and some of the writing was difficult to decipher. I hoped I wouldn't have to resort to opening the original document. If Gram's contribution to the legacy was making copies, maybe mine could be scanning the letters into the computer and digitally restoring them. I could even save everything on disk or a memory stick, I thought with a smile.

Westmeath August 1777

Dearest Sarah,

I thought it advisable to write down my memoir before old age steals the possibility from me. So many years ago, in my youth, Westmeath was a different place. I was one and twenty and my mother and I had just buried my father. As you know, I was an only child, my brothers had not survived infancy.

We had a nice homestead, not opulent by any means, but Father and the farm provided well for us and he saw the wisdom in having me educated.

But now, with Father gone, Mother worried about managing both the farm and house without the help of a man. She began to look to me, not for assistance, but to provide a man for us in the form of a husband. I was well past the age when I should have married and left home. So many young men had left the area in search of better prospects, often in America. Those left were in worse shape than our family.

Mother had a widower in mind for me. He had children in need of care and only a small parcel of land that he could let or sell when he moved in with us. She certainly had my future planned out!

I did not love him. He was a cold sort of man and was nineteen years my senior. The thought of that kind of marriage left me feeling buried alive.

I wanted a love like King Solomon and the Queen of Sheba, Odysseus and Penelope, or Pamela and Mr. B.

I knew there were gypsies camped just outside of town, near the river. I planned to seek them out and purchase a love charm, or possibly beg passage with them to a faraway place if it came to that.

I stole out of my room one evening. Mother had invited the widower O'Reilly and his brood to dinner. It was miserable, but it solidified my resolve. I took a small valise with me, just in case, and all of the money I felt Mother could spare.

The camp was not difficult to find. Despite the late hour, fires burned high and trailers were lit. Children ran about as though it were the middle of the afternoon.

I crept along the edge of camp, keeping to the darkness. I had no actual first-hand knowledge of gypsy ways. I began to think myself quite stupid for basing my plans on schoolroom stories.

I turned to head back to the road and ran into a tall, dark man with long curling hair. He asked me in heavily accented English what my business was.

I managed to stammer out that I was looking for a wise woman, that I needed help. He took my valise from me and started walking into the camp. I followed him, hoping he was leading me where I needed to go and not stealing my possessions.

Eyes followed me as we crossed the encampment, but activity did not cease. Music played, men talked and drank, and dogs whined for scraps.

He led me to a trailer that had once been bright yellow but was now peeling and showing wear. A lamp glowed from inside and the door stood open. He raised his hand to knock on the door frame, when a woman appeared at the door.

She told the man, Danior, to leave us. He dropped my valise inside the doorway and disappeared into the camp without a backwards glance.

I went inside and sat where she bade me. She asked what I wanted. I told her my problem and that I could pay. I said I wanted to marry someone I loved, like the true love I'd read about in books. Surely it existed. Surely God had someone perfect set aside just for me. I only needed help in finding him before I was forced to marry someone else.

She retrieved a brown candle from a cupboard and set it in front of me. She clipped a bit of my hair, then lit the candle. As the wax pooled around the wick, she dropped the strands of my hair, one by one, into the flame. Then she grabbed my hand and pricked my finger with the tip of her knife, squeezed it, and let the blood droplets combine with the liquid wax. Blowing out the candle, she told me to come back tomorrow night. Strong magic takes time and patience. I handed her three pingin, which she slipped into a coin pouch at her waist.

When I stepped outside, Danior was waiting. He took my valise again and I followed him back to the main road, where he left me to go on my way.

I returned the next night to find him waiting by the road. The old woman, Esme, repeated the process with the candle and told me to return again tomorrow. This went on for five nights. Each night, Danior met me a little farther from the camp and afterwards, escorted me a little closer to home.

We talked very little. There was not anything to say. His world was not one of polite conversation with ladies, and mine was boring beyond compare to someone like him.

On the fifth and final night, Esme said it was finished. She could not tell me exactly how long it would take my true love to claim me, but she assured me I should do nothing but wait. I gave her more coin, as I had done each night before, and prayed my mother's wishes could be set aside for just a little longer.

When Danior and I parted that evening, he handed me a bundle the size of a small apple, wrapped in burlap. Inside was an intricately carved butterfly. He said it was beautiful and wanted to fly away and be free, like me.

The next night when I left the house, it was only to meet Danior.

No one could dissuade us. Not my mother and not Esme, who warned Danior was not the one for me. But I was blinded by what I felt was love and Danior could see quite clearly his future as a husband and landowner.

We married, and your father was born soon after.

Did my true love ever make an appearance? I soon discovered Danior was not the love I was looking for, but by then it was far too late. As for the man who should have been mine, there were several possibilities; the new schoolteacher; the man who took over the dry goods store; or perhaps the man who came to town to take the census. I was a new mother and virtuous wife, no longer in a position to find out.

Your grandfather and I had a good life. He was kind to me, and we were good friends. Though I often longed for more, our marriage gave me your father and eventually his sister, and it gave me you. God blessed our land and our family for many years.

This brings us to you, my dear Sarah, and your experiences. When you first came to me, your story was fantastic. You were dreaming or having a waking episode.

Then you brought your book to show me, and I was there with you. I could not blame a dream for the experience we shared. We were Lilliputians. I had no answers then, I have little more now.

I told Danior. He recognized the gypsy magic. He said we must seek them out again, even though he had tried to put that life behind him forever. He feared you were cursed. Your grandfather loved you so, Sarah. He would move heaven and earth to protect you.

You stopped reading Gulliver's Travels, *and in autumn, gypsies once again camped by the river. We went together, the three of us, in early evening. Esme was there, looking very much the same, though her trailer appeared shabbier.*

She said that because the magic I had purchased had gone unused, it had passed to you, Sarah, the next female in my line since you had been born a few months before your Aunt Evelyn. She could not say why you found yourself in the narrative of your book and she would not allow us to show her.

The only suggestion she would offer was to fulfill the magic. As an already married woman, that was impossible, and I told her so. She said maybe one of my daughters would do it one day. We left the camp even more discouraged than when we'd arrived.

I know you remember all of this. It was a troubling and momentous time in your life. I write now for me as much as for you. Later, you can correct all the things I have gotten wrong.

Everything became clearer not long after. We were visiting Dublin and lunched at a small pub. There, behind the bar, was your Gulliver! You had not dared pick up any book in the past year. You had previously read of Gulliver's Travels *and did not dare risk returning to the dangers of that story. But both your mind and your heart recognized the barkeep right away.*

You went right back to our hotel and opened the book. The barkeep was *Gulliver. The only possibility we could discern was that he was your true love. When we returned to the pub the next day, you approached him. The idea of love at first sight is not generally taken seriously. In my experience, it was not to be trusted.*

This confirmation of what Esme told us was all you needed to allow yourself to open your heart to him, your William.

I love you, my Sarah. I'm so glad to hear you and William are happy in America. My congratulations on the birth of your son. Keep this letter safe for me. One day it will be a grand tale to tell your own grandchildren. Write when you are able.

All my love,
Gr. Elizabeth

Chapter 6

In Which the Plot Thickens

It was pretty much as Biddy had said—gypsy curse, or gift, or magic. Whatever. It worked out well enough for Sarah, apparently. She didn't have to spend her time convincing Gulliver he was really William. It's a good thing too. I'd seen that movie, and it was not anywhere I'd want to be. Elizabeth never did mention what specific character Sarah took on. I don't recall there being many women in that book. I suppose it's not important in the long run.

Did I want to delve into the next one tonight? Why not? It was only eleven, and with the shop still closed, all I had to look forward to tomorrow was more cleaning and inventory. I'd rather have my situation sorted out to some extent before surrounding myself with books again. I picked up the next letter.

Georgia, June 1817

Dear Margaret,

I will share with you some of your family history to read when you are older, a most peculiar series of events that are truly beyond belief. I would not even have believed them myself if they had not happened to me.

I am also enclosing a letter that my grandmother, Elizabeth, wrote to me near the end of her life. I won't repeat the information she shares, for it explains the circumstances precisely. I simply want to follow up by saying your Grandfather William has been the love of my life. For all of the mystery and magic (yes, I said magic) that brought us together, I truly believe God's hand was at work.

I want to advise you not to rush into marriage. Elizabeth, too, would caution you on that. Wait for a Godly man who will cherish you. Pray for discernment and wisdom in finding the right mate.

I intend to make my wishes known elsewhere, but I want to tell you here as well. As my only granddaughter, I want you to have my wedding ring when I pass. There will be other things too, but the most important is the ring and this letter. May my final words to you comfort you when I am gone.

Sarah

Postscript, Nov. 1825

It turns out my story isn't over after all. Your grandfather William has been gone several years now; God rest his soul. Until recently, I wore his ring, the one I will give to you. As I have aged, my body has grown frail, as old bodies tend to do, and my fingers have lost their fleshiness. I feared my precious ring would slip off and be lost forever.

I removed it to a safe place in my jewelry case. That evening, when I began my nightly reading, I was, once again, transported into my book. At this stage in my life, I was grateful to find myself in the body of Naomi, in Bethlehem rather than in Gulliver's world. Your grandfather wasn't there, of course, but when I first realized what had happened, I did have hope to see him again. Alas, I was merely a visitor this time.

I didn't know for certain what caused me to travel again. Was it the absence of my William? No. I had no mission this time, my one true love had come and gone.

I now wear my wedding ring on a stout chain around my neck and will do so until I die. It seems to allow me to stay in this world while reading about another. The traveling is just too painful knowing William isn't there waiting for me.

I am telling you all of this because I fear it may one day be important to you. Grandmother and I thought the magic ended when I married William, fulfilling its purpose. Why, then, am I still able to travel?

I will watch you for signs as you become a young woman but leave these letters in the event the magic comes to you sometime after I pass on. It seems you can wear your wedding ring, or perhaps only mine, to stop the magic from taking you; another reason for you to have it. I pray this dies with me and you find your true love in the normal way. I would also advise you to consult someone with knowledge of such things if the magic comes to you. I know the church frowns upon all forms of witchcraft, but I don't think a pastor would ever believe this story, and therefore be unable to offer a practical solution. Be in prayer.

Sarah

The plot thickens, I thought. This would really make an excellent novel if it weren't happening to me for real. I moved on to the next letter.

Georgia, May 1872

Hazel,

My grandmother died on a Sunday morning. She passed silently and instantly in the middle of worship. My mother thought she was deeply in prayer, or perhaps asleep, so did not disturb her until the end of service.

By then, my world had changed forever.

It will be easier for me to move forward with my tale if you pause here and read the other two letters I've enclosed. And I beg you, put on my ring immediately. It cannot be lost...

I hope you have done as I've instructed. I shall continue.

We were at Sunday morning worship. The pastor's sermon was on the evils of fornication, citing the history of King David and Bathsheba, the wife of a soldier. Pastor Wilson always leaves out the intriguing bits about the evils which we are to avoid, so I opened 2 Samuel to read it for myself.

Instantly, I was Bathsheba, naked at my bath! I could not escape. King David sent for me and the story played out exactly as written!

I was nineteen, sitting in the middle of church, my grandmother had just entered the great beyond, and I had lost my innocence to a complete stranger! Only in my mind, thankfully, but the experience was so disturbing I thought I had completely lost my mind as well as my virtue.

The strangest part was, that I was Bathsheba. While part of me had denied what was happening, another part of me was honored to be chosen by the king and fell in love with him, just like Bathsheba did.

The following week was filled with chaos, planning grandmother's funeral, cleaning and re-purposing the rooms she'd used in our home, and of course, mourning. The letters, the ones you have hopefully read by now, were found and turned over to me. I read them eagerly and with astonishment. This is what I learned: First, the magic did not end with my grandmother, it is very much alive. Second, only her wedding ring will keep you from losing yourself in a book, and then, only after you are married. Third, it is possible that the magic can only be fulfilled with Elizabeth's missing true love or his descendant. Finally, there is no way to predict or cause that to happen.

Now that I had this new information from Sarah, I was less anxious about my situation. I was relieved to know my sanity was still intact, but still worried about the possibility of a virgin birth. I did remember that part of the story from the sermon. I wasn't sure if any of my book experiences transferred to my real world.

I knew I needed to find King David as soon as possible, so I delved back into 2 Samuel. The king had my husband killed and we married. I experienced the swelling of impending motherhood and still had no clues to where my 'David' could be found.

At last, there he was. We were in Troy, New York, visiting Rensselaer Polytechnic Institute with my older brother. Edward was the young man leading our tour group. I'm sure he thought me strange, what with the way I stared at him. Later, he admitted to being embarrassed that such a pretty and oddly familiar girl had taken notice of him.

For my part, I was now face to face with the living man I had shared marital intimacies with; I'm sure I was more embarrassed.

When I got back to the hotel, I read myself back into 2 Samuel. This experience was vastly different than Sarah's or Elizabeth's, I had no direction.

I hoped that if I could make Edward aware of

himself in my dream state, he'd remember the shared past of our alter identities. If he was meant to be my one true love, the rest should come easily. At the very least, I hoped he would feel obligated to make an honest woman out of me.

By now, I realized there would be no virgin birth by my waking self, but I surely didn't want to experience childbirth as Bathsheba either. Edward would have to come around to the awkward situation quickly.

When I read back in to 2 Samuel *this time, Edward recognized me instantly, but was beyond confused. I explained as best I could, and insisted we meet the next day before my family returned to Georgia.*

The next morning when they went back to RPI, I pleaded ill and stayed behind at the hotel. Edward met me in the restaurant downstairs. We were strangers, yet knew each other so well. He could depend on my love for him and I could depend on his feelings of duty and responsibility. It was a start.

After much discussion, I insisted he finish his final year and earn his degree so he would be able to provide for us. We fabricated a conceivable courtship story, exchanged addresses, and he promised to come visit in the summer when classes were through.

He then hurried back to campus to quickly establish a bosom friendship with my brother that would allow him plausible access to me. I avoided 2 Samuel *and was pleased to discover that as long as my alter-self was occupied in one narrative, my waking self was free to read other books of the* Holy Bible *and other secular writings.*

Edward and I corresponded in secret till

summertime and became engaged before he and my brother started the fall semester. We married the following summer, I slipped on Sarah's ring, and lived uneventfully ever after. I was finally able to finish 2 Samuel.

Another thing I would like to add to the wisdom collected in these letters, the travelling does not cease simply because you are married to your true love. When I was pregnant with your father, my fingers swelled uncomfortably. I removed my rings, lest they require cutting to remove them later. That very day, your grandfather and I found ourselves immersed in The Scarlet Letter. *After that, when I was ringless, I chose my reading material more carefully, or chose to refrain altogether.*

I hope these letters come to you in time to prepare you. I'll do my best to deliver them when you are old enough. It looks like the curse is part of our family legacy now. Be sure to pass on the letters to your own granddaughter, it appears to skip a generation.

All my love,
Grandmother Margaret

Chapter 7

It's as if Gram Thinks I Have a Lot of Free Time

That explained the Bible. Poor Margaret, how horrible. No wonder she considered it a curse. The other two books were probably added by Gram and Hazel.

It was nearly midnight now, might as well finish it out. I picked up the next letter, the one from Hazel.

December 1936
My Little Mabel,
As I watch you play with your dolls, I can't believe I'm sitting down to write you this letter. I want you to be prepared for what might come, in case I'm not around to tell you myself.

I was more fortunate than my grandmother, who had the family legacy come upon her by surprise. She wanted to make sure I was well prepared.

I know this doesn't make any sense right now. If you are reading this, and I am gone, please stop here and read the other letters I've included. They are from your great-grandmothers.

When I was fifteen, my grandmother, Margaret, told me about our legacy, though she referred to it as a curse. She showed me all the letters, and we discussed what reading material I should be thinking about. She didn't want me to have an experience like hers.

She considered allowing me to book walk with her to guide me, but in the end decided not to risk altering my path to finding true love.

When she passed from this world, I was ready. After I had mourned sufficiently (we were very close), I picked up my copy of Pride and Prejudice *for the second time. Grandmother and I decided together that this would be a safely modest narrative in which to meet my future husband.*

She warned me to read only when I was alone in the house because she had discovered that if there were multiple characters in the book, they would sometimes be filled by real people nearby. Sometimes they were aware and sometimes not. It could make for some uneasy explanations. I certainly did not want my real father and mother appearing in my romance as Mr. and Mrs. Bennett.

Your grandfather, Albert, proved to be slow to come about. After finishing Pride and Prejudice, *I was forced to move on to* Sense and Sensibility, *then* Emma. *It was not until midway through* Jane Eyre *that I was able to discover Albert's true name and location.*

Ultimately, he came and found me. He was employed as a designer for Henry Ford in Detroit. We eloped the very evening he arrived in Charleston. When my Albert set his mind to something, he's full steam ahead. My parents were fit to be tied. It was many years before they accepted Albert and our marriage. In that, I regret our impetuousness. Giving birth to your father and naming him after my father certainly helped. That, and the new motor car Albert gave them for their 25th wedding anniversary.

Albert and I have had many happy years together, and hopefully will have many more to enjoy with you, Mabel, dear. I choose to see our legacy as a gift rather than a curse. I hope circumstances allow you to do the same.

Grandmother Margaret was able to leave some practical advice you read in her letter. I will try to do the same. I already told you about people nearby accidentally book walking with you. Be careful of that! Though it might be fun to take a good friend with you, if you have one who is trustworthy and like a sister to you. I never did, but it sounds like a grand idea.

Oh, and no time passes in the real world while you are "walking,"—you may have already gathered that. When you become a teenager, I will do my best to steer you toward appropriate reading material. That way, if you already like the right kinds of books, I won't have to worry about you waking up in Johnny Tremain *or* The Time Machine. *Neither being a setting for romance and the things you may witness could seriously corrupt your peace of mind.*

Sweet, sweet Mabel, I wish for you a wonderful, happy life, filled with more love than you can imagine. Live well, my darling.

All my love,
Grandma Hazel

Oh, Gram, I thought sadly. No wonder you were so insistent about me running the shop; you needed me to find the letters. I stifled a yawn and got up to get a glass of water and stretch. All that was left was to finish Gram's letter. I cleaned up the kitchen and stored the leftover pizza, allowing the new information time to find a place to settle in my mind.

I fought against the notion that the handsome lieutenant was to be my husband. Right now, marriage sounded like a boring death sentence. I exaggerate, but there were a lot of things I wanted to do before I settled down to mundane married life, even if it was to be blissful with my true love.

I wanted to travel to...places and do...things. I just hadn't had time to narrow down the specifics. Wait! Snorkeling! I wanted to snorkel on the Great Barrier Reef, and ah, hike the Appalachian Trail. Heck, I wanted to go back to school and earn a degree in something I was actually interested in. I needed more time to figure out what that might be. I had lots of plans, tons, that didn't involve settling down.

I snuggled back into Gram's couch and returned to her letter.

I hope you read the other letters, Penelope, otherwise the remainder of this won't make a lick of sense.

I found your grandfather in Breakfast at Tiffany's, *but him being a stubborn one, it took three more books before I finally figured out who he was. Even then, Estelle and I had to present ourselves in person to get him to believe he wasn't dreaming.*

Poor man. Would have saved a lot of heartache if he'd come around sooner. It took over a year. He'd been engaged to be married to his high school sweetheart in just two months, but when he met me in person, that all went out the window.

Okay, now for the advice part. Life happens. Being your true love won't keep a man from marrying someone else in the meantime. It happens all the time.

One of the reasons the divorce rate is so high—people are impatient. You will always meet your true love eventually in life, the legacy simply speeds up the process (that's more of a theory than advice). If Elizabeth hadn't been in such a rush, her young man might have been right around the corner. Of course, I understand her urgency. I might have rushed into marriage too had I been staring down the barrel at an old man and his unruly urchins.

You have to read a book, a real one, Penelope. I did some experimenting with your electronic gizmo and it just doesn't work. I felt pretty safe keeping these letters from you until my death. I know you don't read paper anymore if you can help it.

My mother included the book she first met my grandfather in, and the Bible Margaret used, though I don't think it was the actual pew Bible she started her traveling with. I put mine in there too. It probably serves no purpose. You do what you want when it's your time.

Another thought I had, in this new generation of information, is that you should try to find Elizabeth's lost love. Use one of those ancestry sites, or the Mormons, and see if there's a way to find out who he was. I'm told everything is online now, old newspapers and such. It was just an idea I had. Maybe you could find him on the face book.

If you can find a way to track down his ancestor, you can keep tabs on the family and maybe the magic will work its way around to pairing our families up. At any rate, it will be something new for you to include in your granddaughter's letter someday.

Finally, I want to leave you with this thought, don't

be so skeptical! You tend to close yourself off and get wrapped up in your own plans. Loosen up, let yourself be open to the possibilities.

Finding your true love does not take away from you, it makes you the best you, you can imagine. It's like finding the best friend you never knew you were missing. Don't turn away from it just because you think you're not ready.

Estelle (Biddy) knows all about the legacy. She can help you, answer questions, or just be there to listen.

I love you to the moon and back, Penny-pie. Have a wonderful, joyous life. I'm sorry I can't be there a little longer to share it with you.

Love always,

Gram (Mabel)

I was in tears by the time I finished. I missed Gram acutely. I shut off the remaining lights and curled up in a ball on the couch, willing myself to sleep.

Chapter 8

Sip It, Dear.

Monday morning dawned bright through the slats of the window shade. The insides of my eyelids felt like they were lined with sandpaper and my back ached from sleeping on the couch. I seriously contemplated going back to bed in my own room, but it was already eight o'clock and I didn't think I'd be successful anyway. My mind was awake, busy sorting the information I learned last night; weighing my options as I shuffled around the apartment.

I started the coffee maker and headed to the bathroom. I scrubbed my face and sloppily scraped my hair back into a big clip. Returning to the couch to await the coffee, I picked up *Pride and Prejudice* and carefully opened it, ready to fling it to the floor at the first inkling of weirdness. I read the first page, then the second. Nothing. So that proved true, at least; once I was in one book, I was stuck there. I placed it back on the table and picked up *The Murderous Margrave*, then I put it back down. I needed my coffee first.

Back in the kitchen, I checked my phone and found a good morning text from Bobbie and a reminder to myself to take the donate boxes to the thrift store. Ha! That wasn't going to happen today, so I rescheduled the reminder for Tuesday.

Coffee and toast in hand, I was ready for nineteenth century England. I hadn't marked the page, obviously, before Bobbie had taken the book from me yesterday. It seemed like what we experienced had to have happened toward the beginning since we were introduced to both the love interest and the conflict. I chose a spot toward the middle and began reading.

****

The Murderous Margrave

If nothing else could be said about our gracious hostess, no one would ever accuse her of not providing an expansive selection of delicious pastries for tea. Lady Prudence would have liked to take two of her favorite biscuits, but refrained, not wanting to appear gluttonous. Lady Seraphina had no such compunction. Her plate held a biscuit, and a cake, and a sugared plum. Fortunately, she wasn't included in the main sitting area today, but was visiting with a group of younger women by the terrace doors.

Lady Prudence had purposely positioned herself with the group that included Lady Bellweather and several other well-respected older women. This was the place to be noticed. These influential women would be able to help her make the right connections and introductions once the Season commenced, but only if she made a favorable impression. As much as she truly adored Lady Seraphina, her parents were considered upstarts, only three generations from making their fortune in trade, and their friendship would not benefit her endeavors.

Lady Prudence's attention was drawn back to the discussion at hand.

"If the weather remains mild, it shall be perfect for the garden concert I have planned two nights hence," Lady Bellweather was saying.

"Indeed, I should hope the paths of the hedge maze will also be dry enough for touring. I have heard many complimentary opinions of the statues you have hidden within," Lady Compton stated.

"Have you arranged for more escorts? I suspect the young ladies are growing tedious with their own conversation," Lady Fairview questioned.

Instead of coffee and toast in my hands, I found myself pinching a tiny teacup between my fingers and balancing a bone china plate, holding a single cookie, on my knee. I made a quick grab for the plate and carefully set it aside on the table behind me.

"Of course, you know proper young men are not apt to materialize out of nowhere," Lady Bellweather responded, not really answering the question.

"I understand, how unfortunate for you. I had so hoped the evening would be a success for you, you've waited so long to show off your garden remodel," Lady Fairview said.

"Tut, tut! I did not say there would be no new gentlemen in attendance. In fact, I have recently made the acquaintance of Sir Octavian Achen, Margrave of Austonia. Lady Prudence, I understand the gentleman is known to you," Lady Bellweather said.

Deer in the headlights! I took a sip of tepid tea, and nearly choked on it, to stall while I organized my response. How rude of me, I know.

"He is known to my family, yes," I hedged, "but I do not know him well."

"Oh dear, I was led to believe you and he had an

understanding of sorts." Lady Bellweather looked distressed at both my statement and my tea manners.

"Only in his own mind. If he has already been invited, perhaps it will be an opportunity to direct his interests elsewhere," I said, hoping she'd latch on to that idea. Instead, she moved on. Apparently, we would not be taking any forays too far from the original story line. Another young woman sidled over to our group.

"Lady Prudence, why don't you tell them about the dashing lieutenant we met the other night," the newcomer suggested.

This must be Lady Sarah-something. Seraphina. She didn't look anything like Bobbie now.

"Do tell, Lady Prudence. Don't keep an eligible, young prospect to yourself," Lady Fairview admonished.

I glared at Lady Not-Bobbie.

"I had already forgotten," I lied, "we crossed paths with lieutenant..."

"First Lieutenant Culver Eberhart," my helpful friend supplied.

"Yes, that's it. Lieutenant Eberhart," I agreed, "he's just returned from, er, the war in Eur...um, the continent." I quickly gulped more tea.

"I know the Eberharts," Lady Bellweather said. "A fine family, prosperous estates. I didn't realize young Culver had returned. He's a second or third son, I believe, no choice but to buy a commission or take up the cloth. No money at all there. The Eberhart heir has recently married and is traveling with his new bride. She's a sweet girl and has attended gatherings here before.

"Thank you, Lady Prudence. The lieutenant will be

a fine addition to my guest list. Surely he'll have riveting tales of the war with which to entertain us."

Personally, I'd never heard the terms 'war stories' and 'entertaining' used together, but to each their own, I suppose. I felt a pang of guilt. I'd probably set the lieutenant up to be picked apart by vultures, when the poor man probably just wanted to hang out at home and relax.

****

The next sip of my tea was once again hot coffee, and I was back in my pajamas on the sofa.

That wasn't nearly as terrible as last time, I thought, taking a deep breath and stuffing an old receipt in the book to mark the page. I decided I preferred having the real Bobbie with me. I couldn't be sure of Seraphina's loyalty, especially considering some of the uncharitable thoughts Prudence had of her. Bobbie always had my back and she was smart and quick-thinking. Book-walking with my friend would give me an edge.

But did I really want to move forward with this? Gram wrote that it could take a while, so I should start sooner rather than later. But then, what if I find him right away? Married or not, I'll be stuck with him forever. Bye, bye freedom.

Gram wouldn't like me thinking like that. Soul mate, true love. Who even talked like that anymore? Obviously, people who were living it. I'm sure Bobbie and Peter were very comfortable with those terms.

I wouldn't book walk again until Bobbie could go with me. I might even have her read ahead so I would know what to expect. Decision made, I quickly changed into work clothes and headed downstairs.

Chapter 9

Research is Interesting, But Not Fun

"I have a plan," Bobbie announced, slapping a notebook down on a stack of boxes.

I'd been working in the storeroom all day, separating the boxes into donate, inventory, and sell online piles. I'd made quite a bit of progress toward opening on Saturday but was a little light-headed from having worked through lunch.

"A plan for what?" I asked dumbly.

"For finding Lieutenant Mr. Right, of course."

"I don't know if I want to find him yet. I brought the letters for you to read."

"Oh fabulous! How were they?" she asked with concern. "Was it hard reading what your gram wrote?"

"It was really hard, but what I hadn't counted on was the connection I'd feel to all the other grandmothers. They were all so different and had such differing experiences with the legacy...I don't know how to feel about them exactly.

"They all wrote to their own granddaughters, whom they knew personally, but it also felt like they were writing specifically to me."

"Let's go sit down and go over them, you look like you could use a break. I brought you a snack." She held up the Dunkin bag she'd brought in.

"Please let that be a donut with red jelly."

"Sorry, bacon, egg, and cheese croissant. You need sustenance, girl."

We settled into the nook chairs again and I munched my sandwich while Bobbie read through the letters. She pulled out her notebook and periodically made notes as she read.

After I finished eating, I re-read each letter when she finished with it. Their contents didn't seem any more normal in the light of day, but at least I was able to read without the overwhelming melancholia of last night.

"Okay, change of plan," Bobbie said when she'd finished, "since you're not ready to pursue your lieutenant."

"Quit calling him that. It's unlikely he's even in the military; for all we know he could be homeless, living under a bridge."

"Well, it's better than calling him Culver." She made a sour face. "Or would you rather I refer to him as the soul mate? How about just SM? Or TL?"

"Lieutenant is fine," I grumbled.

"Anyway, since you don't want to do that, I thought we could work the situation backwards. That is, find the descendants of Elizabeth's original soul mate." Bobbie clapped her hands together to punctuate her brilliance.

"And how do you propose we do that? We don't even know where to start."

"Contrary, we know exactly where to start." She consulted her notes. "Westmeath, between 1733 and 1753 or so. If the letters are to be believed, each woman's soul mate is someone she would have met eventually in a natural sort of way. Sarah and Margaret prove that. Hazel and Mabel sought their husbands purposefully, so we don't know how they eventually would have met. So it stands to reason, in that time period, Elizabeth would have met her husband near her home. In fact, she mentions three men who had potential, but she never followed up because she was already married."

"But she doesn't mention them by name, only by occupation."

"Remember, one of those was a census taker, so we know a census was taken in that area during the time we are looking at. That's super-helpful. It will include the names of all the people living there at the time, their ages, and occupations. The guy taking the records won't be included, but hopefully his name will be on the paperwork somewhere."

"You're pinning a lot of hope on mysterious records that may not even exist anymore."

"America is full of European immigrants, and researching your roots is more popular than ever. You can find out more about European ancestors than ancestors from any other country in the world. Our chances are really good."

"Okay, say we find these guys; are we going to have to trace each of their families all the way to present day? What about when their lines split, or they have a dozen kids? We could end up 'narrowing' it down to thousands of people. That's crazy!"

"You did say you weren't in a hurry." Bobbie winked. "This is just a start. Look at your family. It doesn't branch too much, does it?"

"No, I suppose not. I think I have some random

second cousins out there. None of the grandmas mentioned having a sister that carried the legacy either, there was only a brother mentioned."

"Do you know the maiden or married names of any of these women?"

"No, but I can probably find that information in Gram's things. Hey, what about Margaret's Bible? Don't they write births and marriages and stuff like that in there?"

"Sometimes, if it's a family Bible, we can check it." Bobbie wrote a reminder to do so in her notebook.

"It sounds like we do have a plan of sorts. I'm up for anything that doesn't involve me getting married in the next few months. I also have a favor to ask of you."

"Anything, you know that."

"Would you mind reading ahead in *The Murderous Margrave*? That way, when I'm ready, I can just read the parts that will help me figure out who the Lieutenant is and avoid the creepy murdering guy."

Bobbie looked skeptical. "I don't know if you can do that. Margaret followed the story line, though she may have not tried to skip forward. But I'll definitely read through it. Forewarned is forearmed. Since I'm the best friend of the main character, the potential of me being murdered is fairly high. I'd like to avoid that if I can."

"Yikes, I hadn't thought of that. I'm pretty sure you'd end up okay in real life, but it's not something I'd want either of us to have to experience."

"How about I just mark the juicy bits for you to read," Bobbie said, attempting, and failing, to wiggle her eyebrows suggestively.

"Um, no. But maybe bookmark the low-action

parts where I can try to have a conversation with him."

"That may be a tip you could share in your letter, if we're able to work it out."

"What's that?"

"That you don't have to read the book straight through; you can skip around. That sure would have saved Margaret some stress; she could have skipped forward to after the baby was born."

"I think she was worried for nothing anyway. It's not like the Bible had a childbirth scene."

"It's hard to say. There probably wasn't a big seduction scene either, but she experienced that," Bobbie concluded. She started making more notations. "It will require more research, for sure."

We worked companionably the rest of the afternoon. I listed a bunch of books on *eBay*, including most of the penny dreadfuls, and Bobbie shelved books and created nerdy, eye-pleasing displays. By late afternoon, we had completed our goals for the day.

"I'm cooking for Peter tonight, so I need to head out. Mind if I take the book with me now?" Bobbie asked as she collected her notebook and keys.

I handed her *The Murderous Margrave*, hesitating just a moment before releasing it. It had suddenly become the most important book in my life. If it became lost, the chances of finding another were slim. I explained the hasty bookmark and admitted to my read-in that morning.

Bobbie looked a little put out at my reading ahead without her. Quite a change of attitude from the girl that was pissed off about getting sucked into the seventeenth century yesterday. "A garden party sounds like fun. And safe."

Maybe that wasn't such a bad idea, let nature take its course and meet Mr. Right the way anyone else would. But as resistant as I was to the idea of settling down, I was fascinated by the magic and curious about the process.

"I don't know when I'll be ready to go back in."

"I know, but when you are, we'll be prepared. Why don't you start working the ancestry angle?" she suggested.

"I'll take a look. Later." In truth, while we'd worked, I'd been thinking about it a great deal. We had more to go on than most, if the letters were to be believed. Most people start with a name and work backwards. We had a name, a year, and a location—at least for my family. We knew there was a census, and a rough time frame for that. We even had three potential bachelors who we could hopefully identify by occupation. My fingers itched to start Googling.

"I'll see you tomorrow, then," Bobbie said, giving me a quick hug on her way out. I headed upstairs for a shower.

****

Later that evening, back in my spot on the couch, I had collected Gram's Bible and placed it with the other books. I fired up my laptop and opened a new Word doc to record any information I found. I also texted my mom to see if she had any family tree information. She sent me a picture of what looked like an old baby book, hers, I guessed, since her name was at the base of the tree outline.

This proved to be quite helpful; it gave me first and last names on Gram's side all the way back to 1853. I had decided to put together my own family tree since I was doing the research anyway. It wouldn't help me find Elizabeth's soul mate, but it would give me a feeling of having accomplished something for the legacy box.

Great-grandma Hazel, or, technically, I guess, great-great-grandmother Hazel, was born in 1853. Her married name was Archer, but she was born a Franklin. After another hour on the World Wide Web, I had her birth certificate and the names of her parents, as well as the location of her birth. Her father was a junior, which was helpful, so I knew his father, Margaret's husband, was Edward Franklin Sr.

I was only four generations away from Elizabeth. I decided to call it a night. I'd attack it from the other direction tomorrow, since figuring out the dates of Elizabeth's birth, death, and marriage would probably be more of a challenge.

Chapter 10

I Went to a Garden Party

I awoke to pounding on my back door. Glancing at my clock, I groaned; eight twenty-five. *It had better be Bobbie*, I thought, as I crawled out of bed and donned my robe and slippers in case it wasn't.

When I looked through my peephole, all I could see was a Starbucks cup. That was good enough for me. Unlatching the safeties, I grabbed the cup and was relishing a sip before Bobbie's feet even crossed my threshold.

"I didn't think you'd let me in without it." Bobbie laughed. "Did I wake you?"

Bobbie was always awake at six whether she had a morning class or not. I was grateful she showed some restraint and didn't arrive on my stoop with the sun.

"I found where you should enter the story next," she said.

I leaned against the door and took a long pull on my latte to avoid having to comment. She continued anyway.

"Unfortunately, you have a brief encounter with the margrave, but then the lieutenant comes to the rescue again."

"Where are you when this is happening?"

She frowned. "You are annoyed with Seraphina's

'nattering'"—Bobbie threw up finger quotes at this—
"and give her the slip. Then you get lost in the garden
and the baddie finds you. Though he had probably been
looking for the opportunity all along."

"Since it will be you with me, I won't have to give
you the slip."

"I think the story needs to play out that way, but I
can follow you and watch."

"And help if the lieutenant doesn't show up to
rescue me?"

"Of course, but I think it will be fine. It can't get
out of hand if it's not in the text. This will be fun!"
Bobbie said with way more enthusiasm than I felt.

"Let me at least finish my coffee first and have
some breakfast. No way am I doing this on an empty
stomach."

****

The Murderous Margrave

Lady Prudence simply could not endure Lady
Seraphina's nattering for another moment.

"Oh look, Sera, is that not Lady Millicent yonder? I
know you are most anxious to acquire the name of her
milliner."

"Indeed! She looks to be alone at the moment. I
must seize the opportunity. Do join me, Prudence."

"I think not. I fear I will become overwrought if I
don't step to the veranda and take some air."

"Very well. I will seek you out when I've achieved
my goal."

Lady Seraphina hastened off with a determined
gait. Lady Prudence watched as she went and noticed
she came to an abrupt stop. When Seraphina turned to

look back at Lady Prudence, she wore Bobbie's face and a triumphant grin. It had worked! Bobbie nodded her head toward the doors that presumably led to the gardens.

I started in that direction while she made her way through the crowd to follow me. I took stock of myself as I went. Once again, I wore a stiff, itchy dress with what felt like bloomers and iron coupling cinched around my midsection. The dress itself was off-white with embroidered vines of intricate green leaves trailing over the whole. Appropriate for a garden party, I supposed. My breasts were nearly spilling out of my bodice; I tugged at it in vain and made a note not to try to bend over—not that I could anyway. I guess that was the whole point of the corset.

A lacy fan hung from my wrist and my scalp was itching. I patted my up-do and realize it wound itself at least six inches into the air. Combs and pins were digging into my head, and I could feel other decorative do-dads poking here and there into the whole mess.

Bobbie met me at the door. "Okay, you head in and I'll watch for the margrave to follow—hopefully I'll know who he is—then I'll trail him."

"Good plan, Nancy Drew. Have you seen the lieutenant anywhere yet? Are you sure he's even here?"

"The story says he'll come to your rescue. If not, I'll be close by and have this, just in case." She held up a long serving fork she must have nicked from the refreshment table, then concealed it again in the folds of her yellow muslin skirt. Bobbie sometimes scared me a little, but it made me feel better just the same.

"Okay, here goes nothing." I stepped out onto the veranda and headed toward the gravel path that led into the gardens. Bobbie seated herself on a stone bench and nodded to me encouragingly. Five more steps and the foliage swallowed me. The music faded and, surprisingly, my apprehension eased. The gardens really were peaceful. The tall hedges prevented me from seeing other people unless they passed me on the same path. For all I knew, the place could be teeming with people, but I felt very much alone.

Every so often the path would widen and there would be a fountain, statue, or flower bed in the center for guests to enjoy, often accompanied by a stone bench where visitors could rest. I took advantage of one such bench. Whatever passed for shoes in this story were wholly inadequate for gravel paths. I removed my thin slipper and massaged my abused foot.

"My dear. I would scold you for exposing yourself in such a manner in public, but since we are to be married soon, there is no harm in my sampling my investment ahead of time."

I smashed my slipper back onto my foot and quickly stood. This guy had come out of nowhere. How had I not heard his approach?

"I'm sure you're mistaken, sir. I am not getting married to anyone."

He stepped closer into my personal space, trapping me between himself and the bench. From a distance, he probably appeared dashing and handsome, but up close...I shuddered. His midnight hair fell in waves down his back, and his equally black mustache was waxed into a submissive curl on each side of his truly disgusting mouth. Various-sized flakes of dandruff dusted his broad shoulders.

His fetid breath made me throw up a little in my

mouth. His teeth were discolored, and the remains of his last meal were nestled in the spaces between them. A gray film filled the gap where his gum line had receded.

Murky brown eyes glared at me crazily from under his heavy brow, and the liberal quantity of gray hair occupying his sideburns betrayed him as a man just past his prime. I suspected his luxurious wavy locks were a dye-job.

He reached up and gently traced a filthy fingernail down the side of my cheek and across my décolletage. Where did that word come from? I choked back a scream, realizing Bobbie never told me what I should do until help arrived. I batted his hand away when he would have let it linger. His bemused expression morphed into a sneer. Quick as lightening, he grabbed my wrist and squeezed.

"It is you who are very much mistaken. I will have what your stepfather promised me. I am done waiting. You will come with me now to announce our happy news, or I will drag you farther into this maze, after which the announcement will be far more embarrassing for you."

This is not real. No one would say such a corny line in real life. I was having trouble laughing at the situation, though, and I wondered if my real self would also have bruises on my wrist.

"Listen. My stepfather does not speak for me. I have no intention of making an announcement, nor going anywhere with you. Any minute now, you're going to be very sorry you manhandled me. *Any minute now*..." I raised my voice on the last bit. How much of a cue did Bobbie need? The margrave ignored me; I guess he couldn't really say anything that wasn't scripted. As he dragged me by my wrist deeper into the maze, I realized my dumb shoes were also useless for finding traction. I lost one all together and tears threatened when the sharp gravel dug into my bare foot.

"Hey, you! Let go of my friend!" Thank goodness, Bobbie, finally. The margrave paused and gave Bobbie a confused look. He must have deemed her a non-threat, for he quickly turned and continue down the path.

"I'm warning you!" She brandished the serving fork, but the margrave didn't turn again.

"I don't think he can go off-script." I grabbed at branches to slow our progress.

"I'll give him 'off-script,' by golly." She ran past me and poked the margrave's shoulder with the fork. He didn't acknowledge her, so she poked him in the butt cheek. At that he stopped and spun to face her. Bobbie raised the fork defensively, but he snatched it from her hand and threw it into the hedge.

"Release the lady at once!" Finally! The cavalry! The lieutenant appeared behind us on the path.

The margrave immediately ignored Bobbie in favor of a scripted opponent. "This is merely a domestic matter, sir. Pray, don't concern yourself. I only wished to find some privacy so that my betrothed and I could finish our discussion."

"I'm not his betrothed! He's kidnapping me!"

"Sir, I cannot allow you to accost the lady in such a manner, betrothed or no. She denies your claim, so again, I must insist you release her." The lieutenant's hand moved to his sword and I watched the margrave follow his movement as well. Most of the men at the party wore ordinary jackets, vests, pants, and high boots, but Culver was in uniform, complete with weaponry.

"Lady Prudence, we *will* continue this discussion at a later time when you have calmed down." He finally released my wrist, and I clutched it to myself, rubbing feeling back into my hand. "I suggest you make arrangements to accompany me in a few weeks when we head back to the continent." He took the path that returned to the house, and after retrieving her fork, Bobbie quietly followed him, giving me a cheesy thumbs-up and a wink. Strangely, while the margrave barely registered her presence, Culver gave her an odd look and watched while she departed.

"Lady Prudence, are you unharmed?" he asked me once Bobbie had disappeared.

"Yes, I'm all right. Thank you for coming to my rescue." It chafed a little to play the damsel in distress. Having not actually read this part, I was unsure of what to say next. Luckily, it looked like it was his line anyway.

"It is a great pleasure to see you again, though the circumstance was once again unpleasant. Do you often find yourself in peril?" He handed me the slipper I'd lost on the path.

"Not until very recently," I mumbled, replacing my footwear.

"Pardon?"

"Um, I've been most fortunate that you have been available to come to my aid once again. How can I repay you?"

"You may answer a question for me. Are you indeed betrothed to that rogue?"

"Absolutely not! I am responsible for myself and live quite independently. My stepfather sought to arrange a marriage that would be advantageous to himself without my consent." Thank goodness Bobbie had prepped me with some of Lady Prudence's back story and appropriate responses.

The lieutenant offered me his arm. "You appear to be quite independent as well as unaccompanied. Please allow me to escort you back to the party," he said with a playful grin that plucked one of my heartstrings. Dang it.

"That would be delightful," I replied. I grasped his woolen sleeve. "And please, call me Penelope."

****

"Hey, Pen, do you smell smoke?

Chapter 11

In Which We Are Not On Fire

Bobbie and I stood watching from the sidewalk as the paramedics loaded my neighbor onto the ambulance. The absence of oxygen mask and the fact that his face was covered told me Mr. McKay and Gram would soon be neighbors once again.

I had only popped into his shop once since moving in to say hello and reintroduce myself. He knew exactly who I was and welcomed me like a long-lost granddaughter while expressing sincere condolences at the loss of Gram. I felt awful about not keeping a better eye on him. Even in that short visit, I could tell he wasn't the spry, capable man he once was.

The ambulance pulled away, and a police officer approached us.

"Which one of you owns the shop next door?" she asked.

"I do. I'm Penny Darling."

"I'm Detective Spaulding. I'm sorry about your neighbor. Were you close?"

"A little. I knew him, but he was friends with the previous owner, my grandmother."

She nodded her head, understanding the connection. "Well, the fire was contained. In fact, no real damage was done. It appeared Mr.," she consulted her notebook, "McKay, experienced a cardiac event while trying to light the woodstove in his shop. The newspaper he was using produced a lot of smoke, but the fire itself was contained inside the stove. The smoke was noticed by people on the street who then called 911. Unfortunately, first responders arrived too late to save Mr. McKay, if that had even been possible to begin with."

"Do you have a way to contact his relatives?"

"I'm going back in to see if I can find something now. His residence is on the second floor?"

"Yes. I have a spare key to his shop. If you let me know when you leave, I can lock the door for you."

"Thank you." She flipped her notepad closed. "I'll check in when I'm done."

"We're not open yet, but I'll leave the front door unlocked. Just yell in case I'm in the back."

The detective nodded and went back into the shop. At that moment, my calendar alarm dinged. I sighed, and quickly rescheduled my thrift store trip to Wednesday.

Poor Mr. McKay. I was in no mood to get my shop ready for its grand opening, when the business next door was as good as dead. It made me sad, but I couldn't see anyone taking it over and keeping it a tobacco and leather goods store. Pipe smokers were becoming few and far between, and the types of leather goods he sold had a limited customer base as well. For all that, it was the manliest man's shop I'd ever been in. The smell always reminded me of "old man," not in a geriatric, minty-medicine sort of way, but comforting and strong.

"Come on, Sis." Bobbie put an arm around my

shoulder and led me back to the bookstore. "Let's have some tea. You get it started, and I'll go down the block and get us some sadness cookies."

I went inside, turned on the electric kettle, and sat down to wait.

****

Two cups of tea, three cookies, and a few sniffles later I was almost restored to my pre-tragedy state. The detective had stopped by. She ate a cookie but declined tea. She found the phone number of Mr. McKay's sister and would give her a call from the station. I locked up the shop next door while Bobbie cleaned up our tea things. We found ourselves gravitating back to the nook, rather than starting any actual work. Bobbie pulled out her notebook.

"We might as well go over our book trip while it's still fresh."

"Would you believe it slipped my mind?" I felt more like wallowing than hashing out my love mystery.

"Yes. And if it slipped your mind so easily, we'd better hurry and capture what's left."

"Okay then, what took you so long?" I asked angrily, "I thought you were going to follow the margrave and rescue me?"

Her eyes widened. "I swear, he never went down the path. I came to check on you and he was already there. There's no way he could have gotten by me."

"Well, he just appeared from the path. I never heard him coming, which is weird, because that gravel made a ton of noise when I stepped on it."

Bobbie started writing. "So maybe the characters don't exist in the book until it's their turn to speak. Other characters may talk about having seen him, but the scene where that happened may not actually exist. It's just script."

I was catching on. "So like if you went back into the party, there wouldn't have been anyone there?"

"Possibly. I'll have to check that out next time. Not only did I not see either of the two men go down the path, there were no other guests outside either. It's kind of creepy thinking about it." Bobbie shivered, then switched gears. "After I left, did you make any headway with the lieutenant?"

"He's definitely interested." The lieutenant was getting his medieval flirt on.

"Duh! Number one, he's your soul mate, and number two, his character is scripted that way."

I felt dumb. "Well, he was still very sweet. Gallant, even. Oh! I told him my real name."

"How did he react?" Bobbie asked eagerly.

I slumped back. "I don't know. The next instant we were back, and you smelled the smoke."

She consulted her notebook. "For next time, I'll test the theory about characters not being in unwritten scenes. And you will see if the lieutenant is able to go off-script and remembers your name."

I looked around my shop. "I honestly think all the customer areas are ready to go for Saturday. There're some things out back that need to be done, but nothing that can't wait. I don't have the energy for any more today."

"Want to watch a movie? We can find something Victorian so you can study up on proper mannerisms," Bobbie suggested.

"Or Hollywood's interpretation of proper mannerisms."

"Based on reading material from that time period," she said, holding up *The Murderous Margrave* and cocking an eyebrow at me.

"Touché. Fine, let's go up and see what Netflix has to offer."

Chapter 12

Meeting New People is Fun

Bobbie stayed only until ten the previous night, so Wednesday morning I was functioning well after a full night's rest. I'd had no memorable dreams, and no early morning coffee deliveries. As a result, I was down in the bookshop by nine a.m. sharp, ready to tackle the remaining boxes in the storeroom.

The donation boxes from my apartment were stacked by the back door, ready to go when I finished sorting through the shop's piles. I was determined to clear some of the clutter out of my life; literally, if not figuratively.

I was summoned to the shop's front door by the sound of someone tapping insistently against the glass. The man on the other side of the door blocked most of the light coming in and kept me from seeing his face. I got a young vibe from him, if his stylishly disheveled jeans and a slim-cut leather jacket were anything to judge by. He was peering through the glass, and when he saw me, stepped back from the door.

"We're not open yet," I said loudly enough for him to hear me through the glass.

"Are you Penelope Darling?" he asked in the same raised voice.

Now that I could see his features, wow. His short,

dark brown hair was longer on the top and appeared to be frequently combed by running his hand through it, as he was doing now. It was a perfect look for him, and not one many men could pull off. His skin was a darkish olive color, suggesting Middle Eastern, or Italian ancestors, but what really startled me were his pale, blue-gray eyes; so uncommon in someone with so dark a complexion. I placed his age somewhere close to my own twenty-three and was suddenly very interested in how this handsome stranger knew my name.

"That depends on who's asking," I replied with what I hoped was a sexy smile.

The corner of his mouth creased in a half smirk, but I noticed it didn't reach his eyes.

"I am Gregorio Loveridge. My uncle is...was Gregory McKay," he said, nodding his head to the shop next door. "Detective Spaulding told my mother that you had a key to his shop. She sent me over to pick out funeral clothes and any paperwork that looked important."

I instantly felt like a cad, flirting with a grieving man. I was really bad at this. I quickly undid the lock and invited him in. His scent preceded him, sandalwood, leather, and something else spicy that I couldn't put my finger on. Though only a few inches taller than me, he seemed to fill up all the space.

"I'm so sorry for your loss. Your uncle was a sweet man. He and my grandmother were good friends. Would you like some tea or something?" Where was this babbling coming from?

"No, thank you, just the shop key. I too, am sorry for *your* loss. My uncle mentioned your grandmother quite often."

I walked behind the sale counter to retrieve the key. "I didn't realize Mr. McKay had a nephew, or a sister, but I haven't been around much for a while. I'm sorry I didn't stop by to look in on him more often."

"Uncle had a bad heart and was stubborn about taking his medications. I'm sad to admit, it was really just a matter of time. My mom was pretty frustrated with him. He usually came around for dinner a couple nights a week, but the doctor said there wouldn't really have been any warning signs to watch out for that couldn't be attributed to simple old age. Nevertheless, I should have been more diligent in checking in on him."

"Oh." *Brilliant commentary there, Pen.* "Here's the key. Do you want to just keep it? I can't think of any reason for me to have it anymore."

"I'll find Uncle's key and return this to you. I don't know what's going to happen beyond this week, but if I know you have a copy, I'll just give the other to my mom and come see you if I need to get in again. That is, if you don't mind." This time his smile did reach his eyes.

"Of course, anytime. I'm actually having my grand opening this Saturday, so the shop will be open, and you won't have to knock. Unless it's after hours. Or Monday. Um, then I might not be in the shop to hear you anyway. There's a back entrance. To my apartment, that is. I live upstairs; the same type of set-up your uncle probably had." *Ack! Someone stop my mouth!*

"Thanks. I'll bring this back in a bit," he said, backing out of the shop, smile still in place, but in a genuine way, not in a "don't make any sudden moves around the crazy lady" way.

"Okay! Bye!" As soon as the door thumped shut, I sagged against the counter. Oh. My. Word. What in the world had gotten into me? It's not like I'd never seen a cute guy before. Heck, I supposedly had one of my very own just sitting out there waiting for me.

I quickly assembled the donate boxes and added them to the stack by the door. My plan was to prolong Gregorio's time here long enough for me to portray myself as a totally normal, intelligent woman. Surely, the gentleman in him wouldn't turn down a lady in need of a strong man to load her car. I was right.

When he returned about forty-five minutes later, I was able to appeal to his chivalrousness. The job took us about three trips, with me mostly just opening and closing doors and the trunk. I managed to learn that he lived in Ashburn, about thirty minutes away, but visited his mom and uncle here often. He had his home inspector license and did freelance work for a firm in the city, but he actually spent most of his time flipping houses.

"Thanks for your help. With the boxes. I hope I didn't keep you from family stuff."

"No, it's fine. It's not like Uncle's in any hurry."

I cringed.

"Too soon?" he asked with a grin, "Uncle would not want us to lose our sense of humor because of him. He always had a smile for everyone and told some of the worst jokes you've ever heard."

"I never saw that side of him," I quickly added, "but I can picture it. He was always friendly, and Gram thought the world of him."

"My aunt passed away before I was born, and they never had kids. I think he found all the best parts of having a son in me, but none of the hassle." Gregorio was smiling again.

"You'll miss him a lot."

"I will. I don't think Uncle was expecting to go so soon, but I think he was ready. He lived his life with no regrets and no enemies, and he always claimed to be right with God. I'm sure he was ready to see Aunt Linda again. She was the love of his life and he always said he missed her every day."

Instinctively, I stepped forward and gave him a hug, which, after a slight hesitation, he returned.

"Thank you." He turned to pick up the suit of clothes and a box full of papers with a pair of shoes on top. "The funeral is Friday at three, if you want to come."

"I don't want to intrude on your family time."

"You won't be. It's not a very big family; maybe a few friends. I'm sure he'd like you to be there. It's at St. Peter's Presbyterian."

"I will definitely plan to be there, thank you."

"See you then." He offered a half-wave with the hand holding the garment bag and backed out the door.

Did I just make a date for a funeral?

Chapter 13

Is There Such Thing as a Pretty Cry?

"What *is* it with the women in your family and gypsies?" Bobbie asked in a hissed whisper when we were seated.

Of course, I talked her into going with me to the funeral. That way it would be less "me going to see Gregorio'" and more "neighboring business owner paying her respects." Gregorio greeted us when we arrived. He wasn't kidding about it being a small affair. I recognized a few people from other shops on our block, a couple others looked like they might have been long-time customers.

Gregorio introduced me to his mother, Patricia, who was just as gray-haired and fair-skinned as Mr. McKay had been. She shared his and Gregorio's blue eyes, but where Gregorio's were cool, hers were a soft cornflower. She was petite and very pretty.

Across the room, I easily identified Gregorio's dad, who was busy with the funeral director. In the room filled with pale aging Irishmen, he looked like the only person painted in color. His hair was slightly longer than Gregorio's, lightly brushing his collar. It didn't have the same loose, finger-waved look, his waves were held in place with gel or pomade of some sort. A small gold hoop glinted in his left ear. He was similar in height to Gregorio, but I noticed when he shook the funeral director's hand, that his completely engulfed it.

Gregorio looked very much like his father, but more like an artist had softened the pallet, smoothed out the wrinkles, and adjusted the brightness, just slightly, to be less harsh. He was fresh-faced and new compared to the astute, worldly presence of his father. The family was called away before I was introduced to Mr. Loveridge, so Bobbie and I quickly went to find seats.

"What are you talking about?" I whispered back. For some reason, I'd only told Bobbie that Gregorio had invited us to the funeral. I left out all the details about our visit and how smoking hot he was. I should have known she'd be able to read the situation like a book.

"Don't even, Penelope. Number one, you only have room in your life for one love interest, and all along you've been claiming not to even have time for that. Number two, a tall, dark, and handsome mystery man is what got Elizabeth in trouble in the first place!"

I was saved from replying by soft strains of organ music. The family came in, Gregorio escorting a woman who must have been the oldest living cousin and was seated in the first two rows. Other people were seated in small groups of two or three like Bobbie and me. The woman from the bakery, three doors down, was sitting with the younger woman who owned the flower shop across from her.

The ceremony progressed typically. Scriptures were read, songs were played, Gregorio's dad read the eulogy. Apparently, he and Mr. McKay were close friends. There was a slideshow of old photos set to music. Aged group photos of fair-skinned children and adults were followed by photos of McKay and his two sisters, and wedding photos.

At this point, Bobbie handed me a tissue. Mr. McKay and his wife looked so happy. Even in the older photos, you could see the love shining in their eyes. They traveled, they opened the shop together, they celebrated their fifteenth anniversary. What was conspicuously missing, I thought, were photos of the happy couple welcoming babies into their lives, but the light in their eyes never dimmed.

The soundtrack changed, photos of Linda stopped appearing, replaced with happy photos of Mr. McKay at his sister's wedding, a fishing trip with Mr. Loveridge, and welcoming his new nephew. As photos from Gregorio's childhood rolled, Bobbie wordlessly handed me two more tissues. I barely knew either man, but I was heartsick at the family's loss.

Mr. McKay's life may not have impacted the world, but he loved, and was loved intensely by a few people. Is that how Bobbie and Peter felt about each other? Would anyone feel that way about me? I wanted to be loved like that, but was the lieutenant really the one designed to do it?

I stood while the family made their way out of the sanctuary. Gregorio caught my eye over his relative's gray head and smiled faintly. I returned what I hoped was a similar smile, while holding a tissue to my face to stem the flow of snot and tears.

****

"Okay, spill," Bobbie demanded the minute we reached my car. "How well do you really know the sexy gypsy?"

"I got him to help me load boxes into the back of

my car." Which were still riding around back there, incidentally. "And we talked about his uncle."

She knew there was more and gave me a look, which I could almost ignore because I was driving. But not quite.

"And I hugged him because he was sad, and I think we're sort of friends now."

"He's not your true love. If you get involved, you'll only end up hurting both of you."

"It was just a hug."

"And nonverbal messages across a sparsely crowded sanctuary."

"You are reading way too much into it. What makes you think he's a gypsy, anyway? He's actually a home inspector and real estate mogul," I embellished and tried to change the subject.

"Did you not see his dad?"

"Having an earring does not make one a gypsy. Or a pirate, for that matter."

She started ticking off points on her fingers. "The earring, skin tone, bone structure, nose shape, general demeanor, and last name."

"I thought they kind of looked Italian."

"Or Romani," she said, making her point.

"And what about the last name, how can you possibly know it's a Romani name?"

"Actually, that I looked up on my phone after the funeral while you were in the bathroom cleaning up. Loveridge is a very common English Romani surname. There are surprisingly lots, like Smith and White, even, so that doesn't signify, but once you put everything together it makes a very gypsy picture."

"You're sounding very prejudiced."

"I don't mean to; I'm not. It's no different than expecting a Hernandez to look Hispanic or a Thibodeaux to look Cajun. In fact, while I'm a huge fan of diversity, I also love to see people who've stayed close enough to their roots that that unique part of their culture hasn't been lost. It's kind of a let-down just being a random white girl sometimes. But that's all beside the point. My concern is in how he relates to you, your family history, and your future. I don't want to see you hurt and I don't want you to piss off the legacy magic."

"One gypsy, over two hundred years ago, does not a family history make."

"One gypsy mistake sure did make your family history though."

She had me there.

Chapter 14

A Lady Enjoys a Ride Through the Countryside

Saturday morning rolled in with difficulty. The sun struggled to reach beyond the cloud cover, but eventually gave up around nine a.m. and decided to have a good cry about it. My grand opening didn't exactly get rained out; I wasn't sure what kind of turnout to expect to begin with. We had a steady trickle of customers all day, but nothing I would consider "grand." Many were old regulars who were very kind, expressing sympathy for our mutual loss, because Gram didn't have customers, she had friends.

Bobbie ran the sale counter while I mingled. Peter was there to help, though the only thing I needed him to do was fix my "grand opening" sign every time the wet ropes stretched enough for it to sag.

Old customers complimented me on the changes I'd made to the shop. A few new customers came in and gravitated to the trendier sections Bobbie and I had added. The reading nook was utilized, and I had to make three pots of coffee throughout the day. Though Peter drank a lot of that after each trip out in the rain.

Sunday afternoon was even slower. I told Peter he didn't need to hang around. Bobbie and I dusted shelves that weren't really dirty and straightened displays that weren't really messed up, and that was only in the first twenty minutes of being open. Our only "customer" was someone asking if the bakery down the sidewalk would be open the next day. We played cards until closing at four.

"I think I have the next place for you to 'read-in.' Penny publications were not long and drawn out, unless it was a series. This one's not, I checked," Bobbie added quickly at my look of alarm. "I'd rather not use this particular section, but since we're so close to the end of the book, I don't want you to miss an opportunity to talk with the lieutenant."

"Why, exactly, do you want to avoid this section?"

"It, like all the others, starts with an unpleasant encounter with the margrave. But since we're already skipping over some of the boring stuff, only a couple pages here and there, you should be able to start reading as soon as the margrave is scared off. Then Culver escorts you home. You should have plenty of time to talk, because in the book you have a whole conversation, and he asks permission to court you and stuff."

"Okay," I said hesitantly, "I really wish there was an easier way to do this."

Bobbie just smiled at me. "I'll be over after my morning class. I'll even bring you lunch."

****

"You'll start reading right here." Bobbie showed me the spot marked with a sticky note. "I won't be there this time, because it will just be the two of you. I wonder if I'll even be aware you're 'gone.' This will be exciting research!" She handed me the book and took out her notebook. She could barely hide her impatience with me as she sucked down her protein smoothie. I could tell she regretted bringing me a sandwich, chips, *and* a cookie.

I wiped my fingers and brushed crumbs off my lap before accepting the book from her. "What happens in this scene? I don't want to go in unprepared like last time."

"The lieutenant's family invites all the people at the house party over for a welcome home party for him. They have fancy stables, so the women walk around sedately on the lawn and the men go to target shoot."

"So we're going to see stables, but we don't even get to ride?"

"Well, you will get to ride back with Culver after he rescues you."

"Let me guess, sedately?"

"Well, that's the best way for you to have a conversation."

"Lame." I hadn't been on a horse in forever, but I did enjoy riding.

"Go to the yellow place marker first. I want to test a theory."

I turned back in the book to where she indicated.

"It's the tea party scene that you read without me. I want to see if you can go back into a scene that you've already completed. I figured this one was safe."

I read the familiar scene, tensing for the reality shift.

"If nothing else could be said about our gracious hostess, no one would ever accuse her of not providing an expansive selection of delicious pastries for tea. Lady Prudence would have liked to take two of her favorite biscuits, but refrained, not wanting to appear gluttonous. She noticed Lady Seraphina had no such

compunction, her plate held a biscuit, and a cake, and a sugared plum. Fortunately, she wasn't included in the main sitting area today, but was visiting with a group of younger women by the terrace doors."

"Nothing. It usually works quicker than that," I said with relief.

"Excellent!" Bobbie said, making notes. "You can skip forward a little but you're not able to go back." She opened her notebook and added those details.

I turned to the next marked section in *Margrave*. "All right, let's do this. I'll see you when I get back. You'll have to tell me if my eyes roll up in my head or anything."

The Murderous Margrave

The lieutenant put his hands on Lady Prudence's waist and lifted her up into the saddle before climbing on behind her...

Lady Prudence and Lady Seraphina walked arm-in-arm around the corner of the barn. The horseflesh within was impressive as promised, but the smell was beyond tolerable.

"Oh shit!" Lady Seraphina said.

"Precisely," Lady Prudence agreed, though she never would have expressed her opinion in such a crass manner.

"It didn't work. I'm not supposed to be here," Lady Seraphina continued.

"You are every bit as entitled to be here as I," Lady Prudence encouraged, though she thought herself just a tiny bit more entitled than Lady Sera.

"I'm sorry, I'm sorry, I'm sorry, I'm sorry!" said Lady Bobbie. Suddenly the sound of pounding hoof beats approached them.

At that moment, Lady Penelope was swept off her feet by a powerful arm hooked around her waist. She was hoisted into the air and plopped sideways on the lap of someone riding a horse at terrifying speed. Before she could get her bearings, a rough cotton sack was pulled over her head. The arm, still clamped around her waist, effectively prevented her from moving, but also kept her from falling to her death when the horse picked up speed.

"It will be okay! I promise!" She heard Lady Bobbie call after her.

I'm going to kill her, I thought, as I tried to remember how to move with the horse's gait, made more awkward by my sideways position. It didn't take a genius to figure out who had kidnapped me. This must have been the "unpleasant encounter" Bobbie had referred to. I should have asked more questions, like "how did I get to where I will be when the lieutenant has to give me a ride back?"

"You have evaded me for the last time," my captor growled, following his script.

The galloping and fear kept me from responding. I clenched my teeth together to keep them from rattling, and under the sack, I could feel locks of hair tumbling out of my updo. Finally, we slowed to a walk and I couldn't feel the sun on my shoulders anymore. I estimated we hadn't been riding more than ten minutes or so. I kept reminding myself, this is a book, it's all scripted, the encounter is to be "unpleasant," not dangerous.

We finally came to a stop and the margrave dismounted, pulling me with him. He continued to grumble scripted threats, which I had tuned out in an attempt to be less scared shitless. He turned me around and pushed my back up against a tree, pinning my arms at my sides.

"No one keeps me from what is mine." He roughly kissed my neck and chest while I struggled against him. Of course, that only seemed to excite him more. He let go of one arm to pull the sack away from my mouth and immediately crushed his mouth to mine. Visions of what I knew his mouth to look like slammed into the forefront of my brain. I wrenched my head away so I could gag and caught the unexpected scent of leather. And sandalwood.

The hand that was no longer pinning my arm was now painfully kneading my breast. I reached up and grabbed the sack away from my head. I squinted at the sunlight filtering through the trees, then focused on my assailant.

"Gregorio?" Crazy brown eyes stared back at me, then they blinked and were replaced with piercing blue ones.

"Penelope?" Gregorio's hands immediately went up and he stumbled back, tripped, and landed on his rear end, his eyes never leaving mine.

"I usually make a guy take me on a date before I let him get to second base." I shook with relief as I adjusted my clothing and brushed hair out of my face.

"Penelope?" he asked again. He ran his hand through his hair and was momentarily confused when it didn't come out at the back of his head, but continued, getting ensnarled in the flowing locks. In fact, he almost looked more perplexed at discovering his hair than at discovering himself ravishing me. "I am

95

dreaming."

"Yes," I agreed. It seemed easiest for now. But my easy agreement seemed enough to convince him of the opposite.

"I don't know what is happening. I do not treat women like that. I don't know..."

"Gregorio, it's okay. It wasn't you. You were playing a part."

"That is no part I want to play. I'm sorry, Penelope. I don't understand what I was feeling. It wasn't me at all."

I heard approaching hoofbeats again. This was not the time for the lieutenant to show up. Not while Gregorio was still so confused. He hadn't even picked himself up off the ground. I peeked around the tree and saw a sight I would never forget. The approaching rider wasn't Culver, but Bobbie, bouncing along on a fat little horse about half the size of the one I'd ridden in on. I stifled a laugh. She looked incredibly uncomfortable, but also hilarious.

"That is not as easy as the movies make it look," she announced after coming to a stop and nearly falling as she attempted to dismount without getting tangled in her billowing skirts. "I'm so sorry, Pen. I had no idea it would take you back to the beginning of the scene...Gregorio?"

"You are Penelope's friend from the funeral?"

"This is Bobbie, remember?"

"What is he doing here?" Bobbie asked under her breath while presenting Gregorio with a smile.

"He must have been next door when we read-in," I answered, not bothering to whisper. What was the point?

Gregorio grasped onto my suggestion. "Yes! The last thing I remember, I was packing things in my uncle's apartment. I used my mother's key since we are storing boxes back at her place."

"Well, he's got to go. The lieutenant should be here any minute. The margrave is supposed to jump on his horse and ride away," Bobbie said, looking around for the huge stallion that delivered me here, spying it grazing a few yards away. "Come on, Gregorio, we've got to go."

"On the horse?" he asked, incredulously. "I don't know how to ride. No way am I getting up on that thing."

Bobbie studied him for a moment. "Fine, we'll exit stage left." She reached down to assist him to his feet. He looked at her hand and sized up her petite frame, then got to his feet unassisted, reclaiming some of his self-respect.

"I promise, we'll talk later," I told him as Bobbie led him away.

"I don't know what's happening, why aren't you coming with us?"

"It's kind of a very long story that I don't have time to get into right now." I could hear hoofbeats again.

"Will you be safe?"

"Yes, I'll be perfectly safe. You do need to go, though. Meet us in the shop when you get back."

"I'll be there," he said, hurrying to where Bobbie was waiting. As Culver's horse came into view, she pulled Gregorio behind a large tree.

I turned around to greet Culver on his gray mare.

"Lady Prudence! Where is the blackguard who

abducted you? Are you injured in any way? I will drive him back to the gates of Hell from whence he came!"

"Lieutenant, I mean, Culver, I'm fine. The margrave fled when he heard your approach."

"He will still be close then. Which way did he go? I will see he is brought to justice."

"No, no, ah, I'm feeling quite faint after the harrowing ordeal. Can you bring me back to your house, estate? Leave the margrave to the authorities. There are witnesses to his crime. I'm sure he can be brought to justice this time."

He cocked his head and gave me an odd look. I had quite completely departed the script. What's a girl to do? I decided a fake faint was in order.

Indecision erased, Culver jumped from his horse and nearly caught me before I hit the ground. Nearly. Lucky it was fake. He picked me up and cradled me in his arms as if I were Bobbie's size.

"Lady Prudence! Can you hear me?"

I fake recovered from my fake swoon. "Oh Culver, I'm saved!"

He carefully returned me to my feet. "I will take you back. Come, ride with me."

He deftly helped me onto the saddle and swung himself up behind me, firmly wrapping his arm around my waist.

"Not too fast this time, please. The ride out was terrifying."

"Of course. We'll go slow. I intended to seek you out today. Whom should I ask for permission to court you? That is, if you are not promised elsewhere and also desire to deepen our acquaintance." His voice was hesitant.

"I am independent. You need no one's permission but my own, and I gladly give it." I turned so I could see his face. "Do you mind when I call you Culver?"

"Not at all. May I also call you by your first name?"

"Yes, but do you remember what I told you to call me when we last met?"

He looked puzzled for a moment, then brightened. "You asked me to call you Penelope."

I smiled back at him. "I have a feeling you're usually called something other than Culver."

"Most people refer to me as my lord; or Lieutenant, if they served with me."

I released a sigh. That would have been too easy. "Of course, they do. Give it some thought. Is there anything else you'd like me to call you?"

He grinned wickedly. "You may eventually call me 'Dearest' or perhaps 'Darling.'"

I couldn't help but grin back at him. I hoped this was the real him and not the character.

"What do you like to do when you're not soldiering or saving damsels in distress?"

The puzzled look again. Dang it.

"I also enjoy shooting, riding, and attending the theater."

"Of course. Silly me. I also enjoy the theater." Movies count, right?

"When we are back in town for the Season, I would be honored if you would allow me to accompany you to a performance."

"I will look forward to it, Culver." I faced forward again and nestled back against his chest. I felt his arm tighten around me and his lips press against my hair.

Chapter 15

You're Never Going to Believe This, Oh, Wait

Gregorio was knocking insistently on the shop door when Bobbie and I emerged from the stairs. Not that I could blame him. Bobbie made coffee while I answered the door.

"Lucy, you've got some 'splaining to do," Bobbie said just before Gregorio entered. I stifled a laugh. Poor Gregorio. How do I explain this without sounding crazy?

"Gregorio, come in. You remember Bobbie from the funeral, and, um, the forest?"

He came in, but just stood and looked at us, like he was unable to fathom how we could just continue doing normal things. Maybe he expected to find us running around in circles screaming or hiding under a table.

"Please explain to me what just happened. I do not believe it was some kind of shared dream or hallucination," he stated defiantly, like he thought we might try to persuade him in that direction.

"You'll want to sit down. Even after we explain, you might not believe it. I'm still a little in denial myself." Bobbie snorted a laugh at that. Gregorio reluctantly sat down. I didn't exactly know where to start.

"Why don't you start with a question, and I'll

answer. That would be quicker than starting from the beginning and we won't bog you down with unnecessary details," I suggested.

"Where were we?" he started with.

"Obviously, a forest sometime in the Victorian era."

He started to object.

"But actually we were inside the narrative of an old cheesy romance book."

"How did we get there?"

"Gypsy magic," Bobbie cut in, imitating Biddy's mystical hand motions.

"That's not funny." Gregorio gave her a dark look.

"It's true, though. It's a family curse, or legacy, depending on who you talk to. I don't understand how it works. At all. But it started when one of my great-great-great grandmothers in Ireland went to a travelers' camp to get some kind of love spell. It ended up going wrong."

Bobbie snorted again. "Actually, Gregorio *Loveridge*, maybe you can help us out with that part."

"Bobbie, I really don't think he can. Is that coffee ready yet?"

"What makes you think I know anything about this? I still have more questions."

"Because you are descended from gypsies," Bobbie said triumphantly while I inwardly and outwardly cringed.

"Bobbie, please don't," I pleaded.

"You think my heritage makes me an expert on gypsies? That's ridiculous! I'm a builder, my father is a corporate attorney. My grandparents were both factory workers after they emigrated."

"Are they still alive?" she asked excitedly.

"No." He turned back to me. "What is the purpose of you being in the book?"

"To find my true love," I said, blushing.

"And who was I, in the story?"

"You were playing the part of the villain."

He looked chagrined, remembering the part he played. "I am truly sorry. It is not in my nature to treat women in such a way. I don't want you to be afraid of me."

"It's okay, really. Sometimes it takes a minute to realize who we really are after we read ourselves in."

"Wait, you do this on purpose?"

"The first time was about a week ago, and it was an accident. I didn't know about the curse."

"Ahem, legacy," Bobbie corrected. I ignored her.

"Since then, I've been looking through the things my grandmother left me to try to find out more."

"It seemed very unpleasant. Why don't you just stop?"

"It's complicated."

"She needs to find her true love before someone else snatches him up, and so she can read books like a normal person again." Bobbie handed me a cup of coffee. "Cream, sugar?" she asked Gregorio.

"Just black, thanks. So was the guy who rode up after your true love? How come he's not here too?"

"That's how the legacy works. Like you, at first, he doesn't realize he's anyone but the character he's playing. It's taking him longer to 'wake up' than it did you," I explained.

Bobbie jumped out of her chair and lunged for her notebook. "Proximity!" She opened it and started scribbling. "Maybe the time it takes for someone to wake up has to do with proximity! Remember Margaret and Edward? He didn't self-realize until she met him in New York. Gregorio was just a couple of walls away and woke up...how soon?"

"As soon as I pulled the sack off my head and said his name. So you're saying the closer the people are to me when I'm reading, the more quickly they self-realize?"

"Exactly!" she said like a pleased teacher. "The next time we read-in, we'll make sure you aren't next door. I've read ahead, and I promise, you don't want to make any more appearances as the bad guy."

"It could also be that because he's someone I know in real life, he self-realized sooner. We could be pulling random people off the street into the book, too, but we'd never know because they stay in character."

"Good point," Bobbie said and wrote it down.

Gregorio had been sipping his coffee and watching us intently. "So the true love part, is it the real deal? Are you in love with that guy even though you don't even know him?"

I looked into his eyes. "No. I'm not in love with him."

"Yet," Bobbie added, "History would suggest he is destined to be her true love. Following a different path is what got her family in this mess to begin with."

"My original great-grandmother who went to the gypsies didn't wait for the magic she purchased to work. She fell for one of the guys at the camp and married him. Because the magic went unused, it spoiled or changed or something and was passed down to her granddaughter. It's not anything tangible that was physically passed down, it's a spell or something that's attached itself to my family," I explained.

"Do you want to go out tomorrow night?" Gregorio asked in a surprise change of subject.

"What? Um, sure. You don't already have plans to go running for the hills or sprinkle salt on your windowsills?"

Bobbie scowled at me.

"I want to make up for my behavior this morning, even though it wasn't really me."

"Heartbreak! It's the road to heartbreak," Bobbie announced.

I glanced at her, then back at Gregorio.

"Just as friends. We're going to be neighbors for a time, I'd like to get to know you better. So far, it's been...interesting," he said with a smile. Gosh, he had beautiful teeth.

"Sure," I agreed, "the shop closes at six, I can be ready by six-thirty. You don't have any more questions?"

"I'm sure I'll think of more after I process for a bit. It will give us something to talk about tomorrow night," he said smiling. He stood and took his empty cup to the sink. "I've got to get finished next door." He looked at his watch, looked at me, and shook his head. "Let me guess, no time passes while we're there."

"It's more convenient that way, yes. Hey, I sure didn't make up the rules." I walked him to the door. "See you tomorrow night."

He glanced at Bobbie who was staring daggers at him. "Nice to see you again. Bye."

"Bye," I said with a little wave, closing and locking the door behind him.

"I warned you. Do *not* fall for him," Bobbie said. "You'll only get your heart broken," she added more softly.

"I'll be careful, I promise. We're just friends. Maybe he has some deep gypsy knowledge he isn't even aware of."

She harrumphed. "Whatever you need to tell yourself. Did you make any headway with Culver?"

"He remembered I asked him to call me Penelope after I prompted him a little. I think I caught a glimpse of the real man, but only briefly. So not as much headway as we'd like."

"There's only one more scene with the lieutenant and the margrave, and it's the end of the book. It doesn't sound like he's very close to self-realizing. I'll start looking for something to read next, something with more alone time."

"But nothing too intimate, that would be too weird. I don't want another Margaret situation. And nothing rough. I have a feeling I'm still going to be feeling that horseback ride tomorrow."

"You and me both, sister." Bobbie rubbed her backside. "I have a couple book ideas to look into. I won't steer you wrong." She winked at me. "I've got to make sure they have good sidekick parts for me too."

Chapter 16

The Normal Way to Start a Relationship

Gregorio took me to a new local Mexican restaurant. The location formerly housed a seafood restaurant and before that, family-style Italian. I hoped the food was good; our town, unfortunately, had few options to begin with.

We chatted about inconsequential things while we sipped sweet tea and munched on chips and salsa. When the waitress brought our plates, we turned to matters closer to home.

"What does your mother plan to do with your uncle's shop?"

"She's leaving it up to me. She doesn't want to hassle with it and knows remodeling and reselling are particular skills of mine."

"So, no plans to reopen it?"

"You and I both know shops like that are past their popularity, and even if I didn't know it, the books reflect it."

"Will you host a going-out-of-business sale?"

"No, I'm no salesperson, and it would probably still take forever to clear out. I'll probably box it all up for now so I can start on the remodel."

"Some of the leather pieces are nice, and the satchels and purses might appeal to my customers. I can take some things on consignment if that would help," I offered. "I don't want the tobacco, though."

"I'm considering just throwing that out. If it has a shelf-life, it won't be worth anything to pack up."

"Hmm," I agreed through a forkful of rice. "I could take some pictures and post them on eBay, too. I've sold some of my nicer back stock that way."

"I would be grateful for the help."

"For a percentage, of course. Anyway, it makes zero money boxed away."

Gregorio nodded in agreement.

"So what is your plan for the space?" I asked.

"I'm definitely going to remodel the shop and turn it into 'vanilla' space. That way, whoever buys or rents it can do whatever they want. I may permanently separate the apartment above and rent that separately, but I'm undecided. I don't want to leave the apartment with only one entrance. But If I don't, I'd be restricting my renters to someone who wants to open a shop and needs a place to live. I don't want to allow whoever is renting below to sublet the space above. That gets messy."

"Sounds like it would just be easier for you to sell the whole thing and be done with it."

"It certainly would, but I have a little sentimental attachment to the place that I'm trying to come to terms with," he said with a sad smile. "So if you could hand-pick your new neighbor, who would it be?"

"A coffee shop," I said without hesitation.

Gregorio laughed at me. "A woman who knows her mind."

"It's a personal interest, but also, if there were cafe tables out front, it might spark business for me, too.

Everyone knows the epitome of relaxation is coffee and a good read."

"I agree. Speaking of...tell me more about your book problem."

"I'm really sorry you got pulled in," I said, embarrassed.

"And I'm sorry for my behavior. Aside from that, it was a bit of an adventure. I'd go back," he ventured, his gaze fixed on me with all seriousness.

I flushed. "That's probably not a good idea. Bobbie has been reading ahead for me and I think the final scene would be unpleasant for you."

"I would always be the villain?"

"It seems likely. Bobbie is always the same character and the lieutenant is always the same guy."

"Ah, yes. Your true love."

What could I say? The waitress saved me from speaking by arriving with the check. Gregorio paid and we left.

"That place won't last long," I said, relieved to change the subject.

"Oh, why so?"

"They didn't offer us free sopapillas and their mints are subpar," I replied, crunching away at the offending candy.

He laughed and, to my surprise, casually took my hand. "I'm stuffed though. Walk with me for a while, or I'm afraid I'll go to bed with this undigested." He patted what I suspected was actually a fine six-pack.

I fell into step beside him, my hand warm in his. Sunset was still about an hour away; a walk would be harmless. We followed the sidewalk until we picked up the walking path by the library that looped around a small park.

"Tell me about your family legacy. Have all your grandmothers found their husbands this way?"

"It skips a generation, or at least works out so the legacy doesn't pass until the grandmother who currently holds it, passes on." My nose tingled and I blinked away a tear for Gram. "Except for the first granddaughter. Elizabeth, the first one, was still alive, but not susceptible since she married Danior, the man from the gypsy camp."

Gregorio just smiled at me. "Yes, the evil gypsy man," he joked. "Why did it not pass to Elizabeth's daughter?"

"Not evil. I honestly think he loved Elizabeth, but the idea of being a landowner also attracted him. I suspect, because Sarah, the granddaughter was the next female in Elizabeth's line that lived. She was born a few months before Elizabeth's only living daughter, Evelyn." Thinking back, I added, "Every other generation that wasn't a daughter, was a son, until my mother was born, but it didn't pass to her. So it really requires the death of the current curse-holder, and for the next female in line to not be married."

"Tell me about your family. Where did your parents meet?" I asked him.

"My father is a bit older than my mother. He was already practicing law in the city. My mother had her first job working at an office supplier, something like the precursor to Kinko's, while she was attending community college. He was new to the firm and was often sent to run errands for the partners. He frequently crossed paths with my mother, who was quite beautiful, and the rest, as we say, is history."

"That's romantic. How about your grandparents? You said they were immigrants?"

Gregorio frowned faintly. "Their story is less romantic. They, and many others were discriminated against in Hungary and emigrated to the United States with my father in search of a better life. They were treated little better here, and both ended up working long hours in factories. It took a great toll on my grandfather's health; he died before my parents met."

"How did your father overcome all that to become a successful lawyer?"

"Perseverance, determination, and an incredibly high I.Q. He did not want to be left without choices. He shed much of his culture and heritage and worked hard. He was lucky, in that his high grades opened many doors for him. As sad as his parents' lives were here, the best thing they could have done for him was bring him to America. He took care of my grandmother for many years after he became successful. She lived with us until she died when I was ten."

"You said they were discriminated against because they were gypsies? Did they truly live that lifestyle in Hungary?"

"I honestly do not know. My grandmother respected my father's choices and left that part of her life behind."

"You have to admit, though, your dad has a definite look about him," I said with a smile.

"He got the piercing after my grandmother died. I think he was conflicted about setting aside that part of himself but wouldn't have changed anything. He made a good life for our family."

"What about you? I know you were close with your

uncle, but do you know much about the other side of your heritage?"

"My heritage is equally Romani and Irish. I love both parts but haven't really delved too much into the history of either one. Neither defines who I am, nor has any bearing on how I live my life. I'm one hundred percent American and glad to be born into the dream. I'm free to worship how I want to, if I want to; run my own business or work for someone else, or both. I can do what I want with my money and enjoy the privacy of not having to answer to anyone."

"Except the IRS."

Gregorio smiled. "Yes, except them."

We had circled the park and were nearly back to the sidewalk. My reprieve from the legacy discussion had ended.

"What is the endgame for this legacy?"

"Personally, or overall?"

He thought for a moment. "Both."

I went with the easiest to answer first. "We're not sure, that is Bobbie and I, it was suggested, and we suspect, that eventually a descendant of the Elizabeth's actual true love will be destined for one of Elizabeth's descendants. It could even be me, but we really have no idea. Besides, it's only a theory. I have a few clues from the grandmother letters, so I'm attempting to narrow down who it might have been and trace his family tree."

"That sounds like a daunting task."

"It's interesting, and purely academic. If I were to find the guy, throwing myself at him wouldn't do any good if he wasn't my true love. I don't think we can cheat the curse, er, legacy."

"That would probably invite bad gypsy mojo for

certain," he agreed with mock seriousness.

We had arrived back at Gregorio's pickup. He opened my door and helped me in, giving me time to think of an answer to the second part of his question. It was only about a fifteen-minute drive back to the shop, so I'd be able to come up with an answer and quickly make my escape if it got too weird.

"And your personal endgame?" he prompted, as he buckled his seatbelt and started the engine.

"I don't know yet. History suggests that this is the guy destined for me, but I'm loath to believe I don't have a say in the matter. I feel like I have things I want to do before I'm tied down to marriage and a husband." I wouldn't tell him that I was also inexplicably drawn to Culver. Could I want something and not want it at the same time? At this point, I'd had more meaningful conversation with Gregorio; what if I wanted to see where it went? I wanted to feel free to do that, but the specter of Bobbie's scowling face came to mind.

"I guess Bobbie and I will just keep on reading-in until I decide what I want to do. There's no harm in it, and Culver hasn't self-realized yet, so..." I shrugged, "not really much of a game plan. It's still pretty new."

When we arrived back at the shop, he opened my door for me and helped me down. The big, sexy truck really only added to Gregorio's appeal. If he'd arrived in a car, I would have been disappointed. He kept hold of my hand and walked me to the door.

"Now that I've taken you out as a friend, I'd like to ask you on a date for Friday night," he said when we stopped, and he turned to face me.

"Really? Even with all the craziness?" I asked, skeptically.

"Really, Penelope Darling. I find you interesting. Will you?"

"Sure. That sounds nice." I smiled up at him. I couldn't very well lament the things I was missing out on if I didn't seize the opportunities when they came.

"Until Friday, then." He leaned in to kiss my cheek, landing just shy of the corner of my mouth. I inhaled deeply of his scent that had been taunting my senses all evening. He stepped back.

"Goodnight," I said, letting myself in to the shop and relocking the door. I hurried upstairs, turned on my light, and went to the window. He was just walking back to the truck's driver's side. My heart melted a little, he'd waited on the sidewalk until he knew I was safe inside. Bobbie was right, this was dangerous, but I wasn't going to quit living my life because of a stupid legacy I didn't even ask for.

Chapter 17

There's Fun, and Then There's Fun

I floated around the shop all the next day, glad
Bobbie wasn't due by to rain on my parade. I chose to
focus on the giddy feeling one gets when a cute boy
likes them. Jeesh! What was I, thirteen? I hadn't been in
a serious relationship in a few years. *Not* that this was a
relationship. I was studiously ignoring all possible
negative ramifications and had stuffed *The Murderous
Margrave* in my bedside drawer.

Bobbie had finished it and there was one remaining
passage marked to read. The book was back in my
possession, but she made me promise to wait until she
could read-in with me. I was hoping to put her off until
Saturday, after my date.

Business was slow. I had tons of down time but
couldn't actually leave the shop. I'd brought my laptop
down so I could continue my research. If I was
productive, it would help take my mind off the
possibility of Gram's business failing within the first
month.

I opened up the Word document I'd been
compiling. I had intended to get back to it sooner, but it
had been a crazy week. Elizabeth's letter was dated
1777, so I Googled "1700s, census, Ireland." I then
narrowed my search to "1750s, Westmeath, census." I

came up with several sites that claimed to have census records as far back as 1600. I waded through the internet quagmire for over an hour before I finally hit pay dirt, but by then I was too exhausted to get excited about it.

It turned out, the Westmeath census was not an actual government census. It was a counting by the Church of England to record parishioners. They recorded the names and ages of people living in each household, occupation, property size, and parish attended. Unfortunately, I couldn't look at photos of the original documents, so the names of the persons taking the records were a mystery. Who actually searched records for the name of the record-taker? I focused on finding Elizabeth's family.

Using math, I guesstimated Elizabeth's child-bearing years to be around 1715-1760 based on her death being sometime after 1777. The fact that she was worried about forgetting things when she wrote made me think she had to be at least sixty by then. Two parish counts were taken during that time period, so I tried the earliest, 1730.

Good grief! There were five Elizabeths. Luckily, two were definitely too old, and one, I hoped was too young. That left me with Elizabeth McGreggor and Elizabeth Murphy. Elizabeth McGreggor had eleven siblings: too many. Ding, ding, ding! I had a winner. Elizabeth Murphy checked all the boxes. She lived with her parents, her father owned property and was a farmer. She was nineteen.

I switched over to a site that listed marriages, births, and deaths. If she was still Murphy at age nineteen, she wouldn't be twenty years later on the next count list. Besides, now that I had a timeframe, it should be easy to find a marriage record, especially since I knew the groom was Danior. I doubted that was a common name in Ireland during that time.

I quickly updated my Word doc and plunged in again. I eventually found that Elizabeth married Danior Garvey in 1733 and I found baptism records for Patrick Garvey 1734, Donald Garvey 1738, Lucrecia and Amelia in 1743, and Evelyn in 1750. I found death records for all the children but Patrick and Evelyn. I followed Patrick.

I couldn't find a marriage record for Patrick but read that couples usually got married in the wife's parish. She wasn't really important, so I didn't spend any more time looking for her name. It was almost closing time, and I was so close. Finally, bingo! The Sarah from the letter was Sarah Garvey, born in 1750 to Patrick and Abigail Garvey. Like Elizabeth's letter mentioned, she was born a few months before Evelyn. I'd found the first granddaughter.

****

Bobbie called me later that evening and I told her about my discoveries. She asked if I'd found any information on the possible true loves, and I was forced to admit that once the census taker proved to be a dead end, I'd gotten sidetracked with Elizabeth's family and forgot to look into the others. I mentioned the close birth dates of Sarah and Evelyn, which led credence to our theory about how the legacy passed from one girl to the next.

She suggested getting together Friday night, so I had to tell her about my date. Her silent censure was deafening.

"Please understand," I pleaded. "I want to have normal experiences before I get tied down."

"I don't know why you'd want to experience heartache," she snapped, "and what about Gregorio, what about his feelings?"

"He knows about the curse."

"Legacy."

"He knows about the *legacy*. Should I just not have any friends ever?"

"Don't be so melodramatic. An official date with Gregorio is not something casual friends do. Peter and I will go with you."

"What?!"

"We'll double date. It will be fun, and I'll be able to help you guard your heart," Bobbie said with finality.

And so I called Gregorio and explained that our date would now be a chaperoned affair.

****

"So that was fun," Gregorio said as he drove me home from our double date. Bobbie barely let me out of her sight all night, but I had insisted on separate vehicles.

"It was." That was surprisingly true. No, actually, it wasn't really surprising. I loved spending time with Bobbie and Peter, and Gregorio fit in well with our group. With the sudden population change, Gregorio decided bowling would be more fun than the movie he originally planned. I suspected he hoped if Bobbie got to know him better, she would be less hostile towards him. In her defense, she wasn't exactly hostile towards him, just the idea of my relationship with him. Splitting hairs, I know.

"Mini golf might be fun next time. Or Dave and

Buster's, though it's kind of loud there," Gregorio
suggested. He really must have had a good time if he
was already planning another double date. Though I
suspected a budding bromance with Peter. Their sports
talk had been mind-numbing at times.

I, on the other hand, spent half the night trying to
subtly prove to Bobbie that I wasn't in too deep, and the
other half over-analyzing how strong my attraction to
Gregorio was. I had to admit, it was pretty strong. He
was hot, but also sweet and kind. Plus, he was real, and
here.

"Penny?"

"Oh, sorry. Either of those would be fun. Sorry if
tonight was a little weird."

"It is no problem. You are in a unique position and
your friend is just concerned about you. I enjoy your
company and I like your friends. I don't mind passing
the time with you while you work out your other
situation. It is so unbelievable, yet I was there, and I
admit, I'm curious to see how it will all work out."

He was so understanding. Why couldn't I just
simply fall for this guy and live happily ever after?

"I really enjoy your company, too. I'm in some
kind of unreal relationship limbo. It doesn't make any
sense to put my life on hold while I work out my
situation, as you say, but I'm looking back at over two
hundred years of evidence suggesting my life is already
planned out."

We'd, once again, arrived back at my shop.
Gregorio shut off his truck and turned in his seat to face
me. "So we'll hang out, have fun, but be careful to stay
in the shallow end."

I took a deep breath. "Yes, because we're just

having fun."

"Fun," he agreed. He got out and came around to help my down, then walked me to the door. This time, he braced one hand at my waist and cradled my neck and head with the other while his frosty eyes held mine until our lips met. His lips were soft, yet firmly commanded the kiss. My hands gripped his waist so I wouldn't real-swoon. It was over too quickly, but that was definitely for the best. Any longer and it would have risked being too much fun. It would be too easy to slide on into the deep end.

"Good night, Penny," he said softly when he'd released me.

"Good night," I echoed as I turned to let myself in. "Hey, are you going to be next door tomorrow?"

"I had not planned to be." He waited for me to explain my question.

"Be sure to let me know if you change your mind. Bobbie and I were going to read-in to the last part of *Margrave.* I don't want you to end up as the villain again; Bobbie suggested he would come to an unfortunate end. I don't think anything would happen to you in real life, but, well..."

He smiled in understanding. "I get it. I'll be sure to steer clear tomorrow if you promise to tell me how the story ends."

"I will. I'll see you next week sometime."

Again, I watched from my upstairs window as he got in his truck and drove away, wondering how long I would be able to handle just having 'fun' with Gregorio.

Chapter 18

It's All Fun and Games Until Someone Gets Killed

Bobbie and I quickly tidied up the shop Saturday afternoon after the last customer left. Thankfully, business had been steady, at least compared to the past week. I might have to consider closing two days during the week and getting a second job. We had been busier today, but not enough to keep us in the black for any length of time.

I was surprised some of Mr. McKay's leather goods sold as well. I didn't expect people coming in for cheap books would be interested in pricey, quality leather, but you never knew with people, I guessed. I would be glad to report it to Gregorio and the consignment was a nice little boon for the shop.

Over the course of the afternoon, Bobbie had filled me in on what to expect during our read-in this evening. The house party would be going to tour some ruins; the margrave kidnaps me, yet again, with the intention to ruin me publicly (what the plot lacks in creativity it makes up for with persistent predictability). The lieutenant rescues me, again, and the two men sword fight until the margrave is mortally run-through. This was a little bloody for my taste, but Bobbie suggested I just focus on staying clear of the blades. She would follow me but planned to stay out of the fray since it was supposed to be Culver's moment and she really couldn't do anything practical against a sword anyway.

"So, no horseback riding this time?" I really hoped I'd get the opportunity to steer, but it didn't look like it was in the cards...well, pages.

"Nope, sorry," Bobbie confirmed.

We retired to my apartment and I prepared us chef salads for dinner, with plans to indulge in celebratory ice cream after the read-in. Bobbie opened her notebook and sharpened her pencil in readiness.

"Are you ready?" she asked.

"As I ever am. Let's do this."

The Murderous Margrave

"Do you anticipate Lieutenant Eberhart to be in attendance this afternoon?" Lady Seraphina asked Lady Bellweather.

"Have you not heard the news?" Lady Bellweather asked, conspiratorially, causing Lady Prudence to quickly turn from the window where she had been admiring the sheep dotting the dreary countryside. The rain had ended while they were attending luncheon, but the overcast sky remained, mirroring Lady Prudence's mood.

"Do tell," Bobbie encouraged, leaning forward.

Lady Bellweather waited until Penelope and the coach's other occupant, a Mrs. Minerva Pierce, Lady Bellweather's widowed neighbor, also leaned-in to catch the latest on-dit.

"Lord Chamberlain, young Culver's older brother, has fallen quite ill. I heard that he may not live. If the worst happens, heaven forbid, Culver will inherit their father's title, Count Fenderess," she said in a way that suggested she was more excited about the gossip than sad about a man's possible demise.

"How terrible!" Bobbie said, on cue, as scripted, but with a touch of sarcasm only I noticed.

"I know!" Lady Bellweather continued excitedly, "He will be the most eligible bachelor of the season! It's not often a title so prestigious comes available a second time in the span of three years. Debutants had given up hope when Lord Chamberlain married, but unless his wife is breeding, hope springs eternal!"

Well, that certainly ties that plot point in a neat bow. No one would expect any self-respecting romance heroine to settle for anything less than a title, even I knew that.

I cocked an eyebrow at Bobbie and she rolled her eyes at me.

"So you're saying that the lieutenant won't be joining us at the ruins because his brother is ill?" I asked to clarify.

"Oh, I really have no idea," Lady Bellweather answered, settling back in her seat.

"Look! I can see the ruins now," Widow Pierce exclaimed.

Indeed, we could see them as our coach rounded the bend. The foreboding remains of a small fort sat atop a small hill against the steely cloud backdrop. There wasn't much to look at, just a tower, two walls, and a small room off the back of one of the walls. The tower was where all the later action would take place.

Our coach slowed to a stop and the three others, carrying the rest of the house party guests parked alongside. Another coach was already parked next to the ruins and servants were assembling tables (from who knows where) and laying out a light repast for when we were done with the exhausting chore of "looking at ruins." I'd have to make sure my next book wasn't so tedious. A more comfortable wardrobe was also at the top of my list, I thought, as I tried to adjust my stays without exposing myself.

Bobbie pulled me away from the other guests, linking her arm in mine so we could wander away a little.

"I think we have several minutes before the action starts. It's hard to tell. Apparently both men will just appear when it's their cue, no need to worry about the details of how they arrived." She was referring to the observation that the only coaches here were the ones from the party and there was no margrave or lieutenant anywhere in sight. "You'll basically need to position yourself over there, near the tower stairs. He's going to grab you from behind and drag you up to the top."

"Why don't I just go up there on my own and save myself being dragged?"

"You could try, I suppose."

"In fact, we could just go up now, and you could hide behind a box or something."

"This is a ruin; I don't think there are boxes. You go up, and I'll listen from the stairwell."

Bobbie and I walked sedately over to the illustrious ruins and positioned ourselves near the stairs so I could slip away when no one was looking. I started to turn to make my move when a meaty hand clamped over my mouth and an equally thick arm banded around my waist. I flew back into the stairwell, my left heel banging painfully into the stone step and losing my stupid slipper. Again. Note to self: make sure I can wear sneakers in the next book.

I sucked in air through my nose, and was instantly reminded that the non-Gregorio margrave was nasty. The swish of skirts below and steady stream of mild expletives reassured me that Bobbie was close behind. In the story, Lady Seraphina actually abandons me for a glass of lemonade, leaving me susceptible to abduction, but my Bobbie was a better friend than that.

We reached the top and the margrave removed the hand covering my mouth and pulled out his sword. He spun me around to face him to he could deliver his lines. I didn't bother screaming. Bobbie promised there would be no kissing and Culver would be right along.

"You have defied me for the last time, Prudence! There is no escaping. You will be discovered in a compromising position and I will get the nuptials I've been promised!"

"Unhand her foul knave!" Culver burst up from the stairwell. The margrave spun me around again and pointed his short sword at my neck.

"She is mine, and I will kill you or any other who attempts to dissuade me! Do not come any closer." The margrave tightened his hold on my waist, causing me to grunt.

"Penelope? Are you unharmed?" Culver asked, then shook his head, as if trying to knock something loose. He focused on me again, briefly, then turned all his attention on my captor. He put his hands out in front of him in a placating manner.

"You're hurting her, man. Just let her go and we can sit down and talk about this."

Man?

He continued, "She's not going to want to marry

you if you keep treating her like that. We're all a little worked up and emotions are high right now. I know you'd hate yourself if you accidently pricked her with your sword, there."

I wasn't quite sure what was going on, other than Culver had misplaced his script. The margrave seemed a bit confused as well and had thankfully lowered his sword slightly.

"That's it, what's your name, man?"

"One step closer and forfeit your life!" the margrave yelled when he realized Culver had maneuvered himself closer. He raised sword to my neck again.

"Take it easy, I'll stay right here, we can talk from here, all right?" At his point, Culver slowly moved his right hand to his hip, glancing down when he didn't encounter the weapon he was looking for. He abruptly changed direction and reached for the sword on his left hip. On the second attempt, he succeeded in pulling it from its scabbard and held it inexpertly aloft.

Something had happened to Culver. He wasn't Lieutenant book-guy anymore, at least not totally. I'd watched enough cop shows to recognize hostage negotiation tactics and when someone was reaching for a gun, not a sword. The fore-written sword fight was about to happen, and Lieutenant No-Longer Culver was not prepared. I could think of two possible outcomes. One, Culver sucks at sword fighting and the margrave kills him, despite the plot. Granted, he wouldn't actually die in real life—I hoped, but it sure wouldn't tickle either. Or two, Culver kills the margrave, but then has to deal with the emotional ramifications of having killed someone. Though not real, I got the feeling

Culver, in his confused state, would not appreciate the difference, and I didn't know if we'd hang around afterwards long enough to explain it. I also suspected killing someone with a sword was a lot more personal than a good old-fashioned shoot out. I didn't want Culver to suffer that on his conscience for any length of time.

The margrave thrust me aside, where I just barely managed to keep from falling over the broken edge of the tower. When I looked back at the margrave, I saw in his expression the instant he realized Culver didn't know what the heck he was doing.

Oh hell, no. I wasn't going to allow him to take unfair advantage. I slowly got to my feet. The men circled. As soon as the margrave's back was to me, I ran forward and shoved. Hard. My stocking feet slid on the pebbled surface when I impacted his back, but fortunately I had enough momentum, and his weight was already shifted forward in preparation to strike at Culver. I heard Bobbie scream as the margrave went over the edge of the tower, taking me with him.

Chapter 19

A Murderous End

As the margrave went over the edge, his overjacket-wrap-thing, coarsely woven and thoroughly filthy, caught on a broken beam conveniently sticking out of the stonework. I slammed into his back and tried to grab the beam, but only succeeded in catching his jacket. My extra weight was too much for the material to bear and the seams tore out, releasing their unpleasant captive. The margrave, who was not fortunate enough to be in a position to grab anything, continued his journey to the bottom of the tower, unhindered. Oddly, through all of this, he didn't utter a word. No script for this. I wondered, had I been brave enough to look down, if there would actually be a broken body down there.

Looking up, I saw Culver, sheer terror and worry were written all over his face, but at least for now, no confusion. Bobbie appeared next to him.

"Penny! Oh, thank goodness. Hold on, we'll get you up.

"Hurry, please!" I called back, "I suspect falling would be uncomfortable."

"Okay, Culver, you're up. Start rescuing," Bobbie ordered.

They moved away from the edge to hopefully

prepare for my rescue. *Don't worry guys, I'll just chill here for a while. That is, until this nasty fabric can't take my weight anymore,* I thought when a small tear started to appear in front of my face. I could see each individual fiber stretch, strain, and finally snap.

"Anytime now would be great," I called.

"Penelope!" Culver yelled, "don't let go of your line, but try to grab on to the one I toss you too, okay?"

"I'll try," I replied.

When it came, I grabbed for it and wrapped one arm tightly. This wasn't a rope or even a belt as I'd expected, but noticing a ruffle, I assumed Bobbie's underthings had played a huge part in my rescue. I slowly started to rise. I was being lifted by pure brute strength. The look of determination on Culver's face was fierce and magnificent. I had cleared the edge when he flopped the rest of me on to the floor like a trout. He collapsed back, narrowly missing Bobbie. Using his legs as handholds, I pulled myself the rest of the way to safety.

Bobbie was on me instantly with hugging and scolding.

"I had to, he didn't know what he was doing, I didn't want him to get hurt," I told her.

She glanced at Culver. "I'll go so you can explain to him." She patted me on the arm as she rose to her feet. She disappeared down the stairwell.

I turned back to Culver, who I was still mostly sprawled on top of.

"Hey," I said. He had the deepest, bluest eyes I've ever seen. I felt like I could fall into them and stay forever. Then he was kissing me. If Gregorio's kiss was like a warm glow, Culver's was an inferno. He poured his soul into that kiss, which was extra impressive since I knew he had to be really confused about what was happening. I appreciated his ability to focus on his task and set the rest aside. I mean, I *really* appreciated it. He kissed my lips, my neck, my ear, all the while weaving his fingers into my tumbled hair.

"Penelope," he breathed, "who are you?"

I sat back from him, reluctant to leave his arms. "It's kind of a long story that I probably won't have time to finish, but I promise, we'll see each other again. Just...can you please tell me your name? I can't keep calling you Culver or the lieutenant."

He smiled at me. "My friends call me Tripp."

"And it would be okay for me to call you that too?"

"Absolutely, cause I think we're going to become very good friends." He caressed my cheek. "Who are you?" he repeated.

"Why, I'm the woman of your dreams."

****

And then I was home. Damn.

Bobbie sat across from me, grinning like a fool.

"So? I couldn't hear anything. What'd he say? Has he self-realized?"

"There wasn't much talking for you to hear. His name is Tripp, and yes, he appeared to be mostly awake. I didn't have any time to explain anything, though. He'll probably check himself into a psych ward before I'm able to get back to him. Have you thought of a book yet?"

"Anxious, are we?" Bobbie's grin widened. Maybe *she* was ready for a psych ward.

"I just want us to be prepared; for when I sort myself out—my feelings. That kiss blew me away. I really can only be friends with Gregorio. Damn curse!"

"Legacy. You didn't say anything about a kiss!" Bobbie smacked me on the arm. "That information should have been first! Was it amazing? Was it 'true love's kiss'?"

I sighed. "It was. It was the most amazing kiss I've ever experienced, which doesn't make any sense. I can't love someone I don't even know."

"The heart wants what it wants," Bobbie quipped. "Did you find out anything that could help us find him? GPS coordinates, perhaps?"

"No. I didn't even get a last name." I was frustrated with myself. "I let that kiss make me so giddy, all practical thought flew out of my head. When I looked at Tripp—thank goodness I don't have to call him 'Culver' anymore—I felt like I was looking at my best friend. He was so familiar, my heart just recognized him. That sounds stupid saying it out loud."

"No, it doesn't. It's romantic. It's just like all the letters said, in fact, you should write it down right now before you forget how it feels."

"How about you write it down for me in your notebook. I am *not* starting my grandmother letter now."

I stood up and headed to the kitchen, taking *The Murderous Margrave* with me. I tucked it into the box with the grandmother letters and other books.

"I just want to give it a rest for a little bit. I need to focus on the bookstore, dial back my relationship with Gregorio, but still remain friends, and finally deliver the junk in my car to the thrift store; it's been back there for a week! Nothing has changed. I'm still not ready for a relationship."

"Keep telling yourself that, Sis. I'll find a book so we're ready when you cave."

Chapter 20

One Woman's Trash

Monday again. The shop was closed, so I made sure the first thing on my to-do list was a trip to Mary & Martha's. I pulled up to the donation dock and a hearing-impaired gentleman helped me unload my car.

"Thank you," I said.

"Yep. Anytime. You can get a donation receipt at the front," he replied, handing me a ticket that just said '6' for the number of boxes I'd dropped off.

I drove around to the front and parked in the lot. It was my day off, nothing like a little thrift shopping to feed that retail urge, but not break the bank. Besides, I needed a summer wardrobe appropriate for a bookstore proprietress rather than a vacationing college student. Ticket in hand, I entered the store.

After picking out a couple cute dresses and some capri pants, I was ineluctably drawn to the used bookshelves. I never would have bothered with that section before, but it's like when you own a VW bug, you start to notice them everywhere. Bobbie's threat rang in my head, "No Reading!", so I approached cautiously. My phone rang, so I dug it out of my pocket.

"Hey, Mom. What's up?" I asked.

"I wanted to see how things were going. It's been a

couple weeks; how are you feeling about the shop?"

"Too early to tell, but I think I like being there. I feel like I'm learning a whole new side of Gram."

My mom laughed. "You pretty much got what you saw with her. She was the best mom, though."

I envisioned my mom crinkling her nose and pursing her lips, trying not to cry. "She was. And an awesome gram."

My hands absently skimmed the titles haphazardly shelved as I waited for my mom to compose herself. Dean Koontz, cookbook, *Left Behind Series part 4*, self-help, *Junie B. Jones*. None of these would work for me. I had plenty of shelves to peruse at my own shop but hoped something would jump out at me in this unfamiliar setting. Stephen King, *NIV Bible, King James Bible, Sewing Made Easy*, Agatha Christy, *Pom Squad Mystery # 17*... well, well, well.

I carefully pulled the thin, yellowed volume off the shelf. I hadn't thought of this series in ages. My mom had the whole set from when she was a child; I'd read them all at least twice. As I recalled, it featured a 50s or 60s era high school dance team, or pom squad who solved mysteries that kept cropping up in their small town. Think *Archie & Jughead* meet *Nancy Drew*.

"Mom, do you still have those Pom Squad books?" I seemed to recall one mystery taking place at a riding stable.

"Oh my, I haven't thought of those in years. I'm sure they ended up on the yard sale or donated after you outgrew them. What made you think of them?"

"Nothing, really. Just seems like books are my thing now."

"Indeed, they are, and I'm sure you'll breathe new

life into the shop and make it a success. Do you want your dad and me to come down for the weekend?"

"No, I'm fine. Bobbie and I have everything under control. I'm sure you guys are still playing catch-up."

"Are we ever! But we'd come see you if you needed us."

My parents were really the best. "I know. But I'm really doing okay. This is just the change of pace I needed."

We exchanged "I love yous" and "goodbyes" and signed off. I contemplated the book in my hand. I wasn't going to open it, or even risk reading the back flap, to see which story this one was, but I had definitely read it before. There would be parts for Bobbie and me, and, depending on the issue, Tripp would be the steady boyfriend basketball player, whose father was conveniently the mayor, giving the sleuths access to various town buildings.

As they say, a book in the hand is worth two on an auction website...or something like that. I added the book to my clothing selections, pleased with my accomplishments for the morning, and headed for the check-out.

****

Bobbie made herself comfortable on my sofa. She had two books laid out on my coffee table in addition to my own Pom Squad Mystery.

"I think this one would be great," Bobbie said, presenting me with a copy of *Eat, Pray, Love*.

"I've seen that movie. Remember, I said no books with sex. Besides, there's no 'friend' part, and the main character doesn't meet the guy till towards the end."

"So here's my thought on this, neither of us can

134

afford an actual vacation this summer, let alone international travel. This would be perfect! I'd show up as some random character every time you read-in, we'd have a blast. You could catch up with Tripp toward the ending, and since he's self-aware now, you could skip the intimate parts and just talk...if that's what you both really want to do." She winked at me comically.

"Let's just set that one on the back burner for now. What else?"

She held up her next option. "This one is perfect! Plenty of alone time, no sex, cooler temperatures, hot guys."

"Hot vampires, you mean. No way."

"Why not? I know you loved this series," Bobbie pouted.

"It would never work. I was Team Jacob, remember?"

"Pfft, whatever. I haven't read your thrift store find."

"I'm sure it will be appropriate. I know there's no sex, and the characters spend time together solving mysteries. You'd be part of the pom squad with me. Tripp would be the boyfriend basketball player. Peter might even enjoy this one."

"But what's the story about?"

"The plots are all pretty much the same. There's a small-time mysterious crime committed or strange happening that ends up being somehow connected to a squad member. The main character, Beth, and one or two other squad members work to solve the mystery. Her boyfriend is brought in either for muscle or city connection, there is an episode of mild peril, then the mystery is solved. It's all very *Scooby-Doo*."

Bobbie picked it up and read the back cover. "*The time capsule from the school library has been stolen and Mr. Louie, beloved school janitor, is the prime suspect! Can Beth and her Pom Squad friends find the real culprit in time to open it at the homecoming assembly or will Mr. Louie lose his job? The Pom Squad has their work cut out for them this time. Will they even have time to solve the crime while coming up with a new, show-stopping routine for the homecoming game, and will it be good enough to beat their rivals, the LaSalle Cavaliers? There's only one way to find out, loyal readers!"*

I don't think I can do it, Pen. It sounds so, so, bad."

"It will be great. I loved these as a pre-teen."

"It's your love life, I'm just along for the ride. You want me to still read ahead for you?"

"Probably be a good idea. Thanks."

"Of course. I'll try not to fall asleep... or vomit," Bobbie tucked the book in her purse. "When do you want to start?"

"I don't know. I'm sure Tripp is super-confused; I don't want to leave him hanging for long. But, on the other hand, I know once I start on this course, I've got to see it through till the end. The sooner we start, the sooner the end comes, and I don't think I'm ready for the steps that come after that."

"Just because he's yours, doesn't mean you have to claim him immediately. You guys can go on real dates for a while, you don't have to get married right away...unless you want to."

"I suppose. It will be difficult if he ends up living in a whole other state."

"Quit inventing problems where none yet exist."

A knock sounded on my apartment door. Since Bobbie was already here, there were only a few people it could be. One being a problem that wasn't an invention. I peered through the peephole. Yep, my biggest complication stood on the stoop.

"Gregorio!" I said, opening the door.

"Hello, Penelope." He leaned in and kissed me on the cheek. "Hi, Bobbie," he added.

"Nice to see you, Gregorio." She rose, taking our dirty cups and disappearing into the kitchen. She managed to do it so naturally, it wasn't obvious she was giving me time alone with Gregorio to break the bad news.

"What brings you by?" I asked.

"Would you believe me if I said I just wanted to see you?"

I cringed a little.

He gave me an assessing look. "Don't worry, Penelope, I just need the key for next door. But I think you have something on your mind."

"I do." *What do I do now*, I wondered; *stand here awkwardly, take him to the couch*? How do I break up with someone I'm not actually dating? Thankfully, Gregorio solved my problem by casually leaning on the doorframe and tucking his hands in his pants pockets.

"You seem nervous. I'm going to guess you finished your book, and it ended with you and the hero riding off into the sunset." He smiled at me.

"Not exactly. His name is Tripp. I don't know anything else about him, but I did learn that the curse..."

"Legacy!" came a yell from the kitchen.

"Legacy is pretty spot-on. I felt things that were unexpected, but that I can't discount. And I'm really sorry I led you on, and I really like you and want us to be friends, but friends that don't kiss, 'cause it was a really great kiss, but I'm afraid it will just confuse things. I'm sorry." My words rushed out.

He pulled a hand from his pocket and reached to hold mine.

"Penelope, it's okay, really. I'm sad you don't want to go any further with me, but I understand. As much as anyone can understand an impossible situation created by magic two hundred years ago." He smiled, then leaned forward and kissed my forehead.

My body relaxed in relief.

"And we have to remain friends. I want to know how the story ends, and I want to see what kind of soul mate destiny has chosen for you. Maybe one day I should be so lucky."

"Thank you." I reached up and gave him a hug. A friendly hug. "Let me go grab you that key."

****

Wednesday afternoon I was holding down the fort in the bookstore. Business was predictably slow, so I continued working on the genealogy I'd abandoned last week in all the *Margrave* excitement. It was not going well. I gave up on the census taker, not having found his name on any of the documents. I was going to cross my fingers and assume he wasn't "the one" and Elizabeth had only mentioned him randomly in her letter because he was good-looking. Him being "it" was chancy at best; he was only in town for a short time and she would not have had the opportunity to get to know him even if she wasn't already married.

I decided it was better to focus on the teacher and the store owner. They would have had more permanence in Westmeath, thus time to build a relationship. Personally, my private wager was on the shop owner. Elizabeth would have plenty of occasions to stop by and pick up a gallon of milk, or whatever, for her mother. She would only see the teacher in passing since she did not have children or younger siblings.

The bell over the door tinkled, and Aunt Biddy bustled in.

"Aunt Biddy! I'm glad you stopped by. You haven't been in since we finished getting the shop ready," I greeted her.

"I've been under the weather, but I'm finally feeling better. Sorry I missed your grand opening," she said giving me a hug and patting my back. "Bobbie tells me you finished your first book."

I led her to the nook to sit down and offered her a cup of coffee. Someone needed to drink it, I poured out over half a carafe every afternoon.

"We did finish *The Murderous Margrave*. Did she tell you about it?"

"Yes, she did. It's a decent start. She says you're putting off going back in." She put the cup to her lips and peered at me over the rim. The statement was made casually, but I know it was really a question she wanted answered, and probably the only reason she even stopped by to see me.

"I don't want to rush into it. I've already said I'm not ready for a relationship."

"Excuses," Biddy said sharply. "You're afraid of what you feel. Mabel told me to watch out for you in this. She was worried you'd be too skeptical to play it out."

"I fully intend to play it out, just not immediately."

"What about that poor confused boy out there somewhere waiting for you? Are you just going to leave him hanging?"

"No. I'm sure he's going about his business. My soul mate wouldn't allow weird dreams and a few questions to paralyze him with fear and indecision. He's out there going to work or school or whatever, mowing his lawn, watching the game. You know, living is life."

"Dating."

"What?" I choked on my coffee.

"Remember, I saw that young man. He was a hottie. It would stand to reason that he's probably not sitting home playing solitaire on a Friday night. You weren't."

Oops. Sounds like Aunt Biddy had heard about Gregorio and wasn't any happier about it than Bobbie had been.

Now that she had put the idea in my head, I momentarily explored how I felt about Tripp dating. Hmmm. No, I didn't like that idea one bit; the thought of him kissing another girl the same way he had kissed me, awarding some other girl with the same smile. Nope. Dang it, Biddy.

I sighed. "I'll probably start the next book this weekend when Bobbie has the time to go with me."

"Good girl," she said, rising to leave. "You let me know if you have any questions. I'm here to help; I promised your gram." She gave me a hug, and I squeezed her back. She was warm and rounded like Gram had been. I could almost pretend it was her.

She toddled off toward the door. "All right then, bye now, Penelope."

"Bye and thank you."
She waved me off and was gone.
I hoped Bobbie had her pom poms ready.

Epilogue

He Said

The Murderous Margrave

My heart stopped as I watched Penelope and the perpetrator sail over the broken part of the wall. I didn't even know this woman, yet she invaded my dreams and had become incredibly important. I ran to the edge and looked over. She was clinging to a rough piece of fabric that had been caught on the rotting remains of a support beam about two feet down. The other guy was nowhere to be seen, but I wasn't concerned with him anyway.

Another woman dropped to her knees beside me and looked over,

"Penny! Oh, thank goodness. Hold on, we'll get you up."

"Hurry, please!" Penelope called back, "I suspect falling would be uncomfortable."

"Okay, Culver, you're up. Start rescuing," the petite brunette demanded.

"I don't have any of my gear, I'm going to try to reach for her, but I need you to sit on my legs." I looked at her skeptically. "Or maybe you should run downstairs and get help."

She waved me off. "There isn't anyone down there, we're on our own." Then she stripped off her pantaloons and two layers of skirting and began tying them together.

"Let me," I said, taking them from her. If I was going to trust a life to a rope made of ladies' underwear, I was going to make sure the knots would hold. We heard a quick tearing sound from the edge.

"Anytime now would be great," Penelope called.

"I'm going to tie this end around my waist, then lower the other end down," I told Penelope's friend. "Penelope!" I yelled, "do not let go of your line, but try to grab on to the one I toss you too, okay?"

"I'll try," came the reply.

I stepped to the edge and lowered the makeshift rope down. "Grab hold of my belt to help anchor me," I said to the other gal. The line reached Penelope and she hugged it to herself, wrapping it once around her arm for good measure. "I'm going to start lifting you up," I called.

I started pulling, hand over hand. "You're doing great! Almost there." As she was raised past the support beam, the fabric she had been hanging on lifted away and hung limply over her arm.

As soon as her upper body cleared the edge, I stepped back, pulling her on to the stone floor. The gal behind me had enough sense to pull with me, then move out of the way when I fell backwards. Penelope grabbed my leg and pulled herself the rest of the way up. Her friend was right there, pulling her into a hug.

"What were you thinking, Pen? That wasn't even an option," she scolded.

"I had to. He didn't know what he was doing. I didn't want him to get hurt," Penelope explained to her.

Even though it was true, I bristled at the comment.

The girl glanced at me. "I'll go so you can explain to him." She patted Penelope on the arm and rose to her feet.

Penelope looked at me then, with the most beautiful golden hazel eyes I've ever seen. This woman, who I knew nothing about but her name, transfixed me with those damn eyes.

"Hey," she said.

I couldn't do anything but drag her into my lap and kiss her. She almost died. I had to prove to myself that she was real and alive, even if nothing else about this crazy dream was real. There was no way, Penelope, the girl haunting my dreams, wasn't real. Thankfully, she returned my kiss instead of slapping my face.

"Penelope," I breathed when I finally came up for air, "who are you?"

"It's kind of a long story, that I probably won't have time to finish, but I promise, we'll see each other again. Just...can you please tell me your name? I can't keep calling you Culver or the lieutenant."

"My friends call me Tripp."

"And it would be okay for me to call you that too?"

"Absolutely, 'cause I think we're going to become very good friends," I said, caressing her cheek. "Who are you?" I repeated my initial question.

"Why, I'm the woman of your dreams."

****

"Like this?"

I blinked. The woman next to me holding a handgun gave me a questioning look.

"Uh, no," I replied, regaining my bearings, I repositioned her hands. "You need to support it here and widen your stance a little. Hold on a sec, would you please?" I called over my shoulder, "Hey, Scott, take over for me here, please. I just remembered something urgent I need to take care of."

"Sure thing, boss." Scott donned safety glasses and ear protection and joined the woman and me on the indoor range.

"Excuse me, please. Scott's going to come finish up with you. He's my top guy"—actually my only guy—"so you're in expert hands."

"This is Mrs. Brooks, a first-timer, take good care of her," I said to Scott before escaping to my office.

I collapsed into my chair. *What the hell?* I had just experienced an entire dream sequence in a split second. I ran my hand through my hair, once again, clipped short with a little more length on top. It had been weird feeling it tickling my neck and ears. Also gone were the tall boots and itchy leggings. I patted the pockets of my familiar cargo pants, searching for my cell.

Should I call Dr. Lane? I hadn't had an episode in six months, and this had been nothing like those anyway. She told me that in many, PTSD never truly went away, but occurrences lessened, and it was important to have an arsenal of coping skills.

I thought back to my dream, or whatever it was. The woman, Penelope, was so achingly familiar. I hadn't dated since I was discharged a year and a half ago, so it's not like I was inserting some girl I knew into the dreams.

She, and her friend, didn't fit into the dream any better than I did. She didn't react like I would have expected to the hostage situation. Who throws herself off a tower to prevent a sword fight? I didn't handle it well either, thought. The absence of my Glock 27 threw me off balance.

I grabbed a pen from my desk and a sticky note. "Penelope," I wrote. Was that right? "Penelopy," definitely wrong. "Penny." "Pen." Pen is what the other girl called her. She looked like a Pen with that wild curly hair and mysterious eyes. I threw the pen across the room. What was I, some kind of poet now?

I couldn't call Dr. Lane about this.

I thought back to the other dreams I'd had about the girl. They had been different than this one. In them, I was me, but also not quite me either. It had been like I was watching myself play a part. I'd discounted, and mostly forgotten about them.

This time I had been all-in. The hostage situation caused all my training to kick in—for all the good it did. I think Penelope...Pen, thought she was rescuing me.

The phone on my desk rang. Carol, the front gal, was out on maternity leave, so Scott and I had decided to cover for her rather than hire and train someone to just work six weeks. This also allowed me to give Carol paid leave.

I grabbed the handset. "Tripp's Trigger Supply and Range."

"Tripp, honey, are you coming for dinner tonight?"

"I can't tonight, Ma. Remember, I'm short-staffed right now, and we're open late on Saturday nights?"

"I worry you're overextending yourself."

"I was cleared to resume normal activity weeks ago." Well, "new normal," anyway. "Everything has been fine; I'm not overdoing it, promise."

"Your sister and Brian and little Gwennie are going to be here. Maybe after work?"

I inwardly groaned. My mom was an expert cajoler. "It wouldn't be till nine, Ma. I'll be ready for bed by then. I gotta run, Scott needs me. Love you. Tell Alaina and Brian I'm sorry I missed them; give Gwen a hug from Uncle Tripp for me."

"I will. Love you too, baby. Drive safe."

I disconnected and shoved myself to my feet. I wasn't lying, I did need to get back out to help Scott.

I'd put the dreams out of my mind and focus on work. But I found trying to not think about the golden-eyed beauty and that kiss, only succeeded in making it the only thing I couldn't stop thinking about.

A word about the author...

Shelley is a twenty-five year resident of Oklahoma with roots in Maine. She and her husband have four awesome kids but are thrilled two have successfully reached adulthood and moved out. She spends her time working with students, writing, reading, baking, sewing, and exercising just enough to counteract her other activities.

Penny Gothic owes its beginnings to time spent trapped in a classroom monitoring state tests. No reading, no cell phones, no laptops. Penny was born the old-fashioned way, with paper and pen.

Thank you for purchasing
this publication of The Wild Rose Press, Inc.

For questions or more information
contact us at
info@thewildrosepress.com.

The Wild Rose Press, Inc.
www.thewildrosepress.com